Old Drumble

Old Drumble

Jack Lasenby

HarperCollins*Publishers*

National Library of New Zealand Cataloguing-in-Publication Data

Lasenby, Jack.

Old Drumble / Jack Lasenby.

ISBN 978-1-86950-674-2

[1. Farm life—Fiction. 2. Livestock—Fiction. 3. Waharoa (N.Z.)

—Fiction.] I. Title.

NZ823.2—dc 22

First published 2008

HarperCollins*Publishers (New Zealand) Limited*

P.O. Box 1, Auckland

ISBN: 978 1 86950 674 2

Cover design by Louise McGeachie
Cover images courtesy of Shutterstock
Printed by Griffin Press, Australia

50gsm Bulky News used by HarperCollins*Publishers* is a natural,
recyclable product made from wood grown in sustainable plantation
forests. The manufacturing processes conform to the environmental
regulations in the country of origin, New Zealand.

A Bit About Me

Dear Reader,

I write my books up in the top of my house, where the rafters come to a sharp point. It takes about a year to write a book. That's why my head has grown pointed, like an upside down V, with ears stuck on the sides.

A pointed head has two disadvantages. One is that I have trouble keeping a hat on.

The other disadvantage is that, working away with my head stuck up between the rafters under the roof, all my hair's been rubbed off. I think that may be why my neighbour's dog, Ya-Ya, barks when she sees me. It's certainly the reason why I spend a fortune on furniture polish, keeping my bald head shiny.

I just thought you might like to read these bits about me. Most people I know are more interested in the author than his books. I think that's daft, but then Ya-Ya must think I'm daft, or she wouldn't bark at me.

Having a pointed head has two advantages. When I stand on my head, the point digs into the ground, so I can kick my legs around without falling over. It also comes in handy for making holes in the garden, when I'm planting vegies. I've tried but can't think of any other advantage.

Yours Pointedly,
Jack Lasenby

Chapter One

Why Jack Jackman
Liked Living in Ward Street.

JACK JACKMAN LIKED LIVING in Ward Street because it was the stock route through Waharoa.

What he liked best was sitting on top of the gatepost and watching the mobs of sheep and cattle go past. Best of all was when the drovers and dogs came cracking whips, whistling, barking, and running a bad-tempered Jersey bull along Ward Street. That was so exciting, Jack once stood up and fell off the gatepost.

After that, he used to climb down and watch through the fence as the bull trundled past, rolling its little eye, and slavering dribble. Once, Jack poked out his tongue and was scared the bull had seen him. Another time, he heard a squelch from a bull's insides, as it trotted past and, despite his terror, he thought it was crying and felt sorry for it.

"When I grow up, I'm going to be a drover," he told his mother.

"We'll see," she told him.

"But I'm not going to chase the bulls till they cry."

"They only push them through Waharoa, so they don't

have a chance to give any trouble. Once they're out on the road again, away from the houses, they'll take it easy."

"Do you push me, so I don't have a chance to give you any trouble?" Jack asked his mother

"I do," she said, "but once you get the other side of Waharoa, I'll let you take it easy."

"When will that be?"

"When you've grown up and can look after yourself," his mother told him. She wasn't grinning, but Jack wasn't sure if she was having him on. He never could tell with his mother.

All that happened years ago, before Jack started school. His place was straight across Ward Street from the school, but when people said, "That's handy for you. Do you like that?" he wasn't sure.

The school doors, the windows, the gate in the hedge, even the big gate into the horse paddock were all shut for the long holidays. The place looked as good as dead, so Jack didn't even glance at the school, the day he trotted past towards the other end of Ward Street.

Jack Jackman may not have been sure about living so close to the school, but he sure liked living in Ward Street. Ward Street was the stock route through Waharoa!

Chapter Two

Why Harry Jitters Said "I Am Not Snot!", Why Minnie Mitchell Looked at the Toe of Her Shoe, and What She Told Jack Jackman About Ward Street.

JACK'S MOTHER ALWAYS SAID theirs was the top end of Ward Street, but Harry Jitters who lived down the other end reckoned his was the top end.

"How do you know?" asked Jack.

"Because my mother says so," said Harry Jitters. "Besides, when it rains, the water runs down your end, so that makes our end the top end of Ward Street."

"It does not!" said Jack.

"Does so!"

"Does not!"

"Does so!"

"Does snot!"

"I am not snot!"

"Who said you're snot?"

"What'd you say?"

"Clean out your ears!" Jack roared.

They were chatting near Harry's place, where Ward Street turns and goes down to the church corner, when

Minnie Mitchell came home from doing the shopping for her mother. Minnie was skipping carefully so as not to get dust on her new red shoes, singing artlessly to herself, swinging her basket with the bread, the letters, and the paper. Even though they were the only other people on the street, and even though she skipped right between them, Minnie didn't seem to see Jack and Harry until she had opened her gate.

"Oh!" she said, turning back, opening her eyes wide, and pointing the tip of one red shoe at the ground. "You scared me! You have no right sneaking up on people." She tossed her carefully made curls.

Because he had grown up next door to Minnie, and knew better than to argue with her, Harry was silent. Jack, though, was annoyed.

"I did not sneak up!" he said.

Minnie ignored him and looked at Harry. "What were you two arguing about?" she asked.

Harry was eager to explain. "He reckons his end's the top end of—" he started to say, but Minnie cut him off.

"You live down the bottom end of Ward Street, Jack Jackman," she said crisply. Minnie could be very crisp. "Everybody knows that. So there!"

"Yeah!" said Harry. "Everybody knows that."

"It's nicer up the top end of Ward Street." Minnie put down her basket, smiled at the toe of one new red shoe, and patted her curls. "My mother says they're a better class of people up our end, the residential end."

"Yeah!" said Harry. "You live down the school end."

"You'd better go back down your end of the street, Jack Jackman," said Minnie Mitchell. She screwed her head over her shoulder to look at the back of her shoes, the way she'd seen her mother checking the seams of her stockings before she went out. "We don't want your sort up here: you belong down the bottom end. So there!"

Chapter Three

Why Mrs Mitchell Jumped Up and Down, Why Harry Stood With His Head Tipped Well Back, and How Jack's Mother Knew Everything He Was Up To.

"SOME DAY," Minnie Mitchell told Jack Jackman crisply, "my mother says, some day they're going to change the stock route through Waharoa. They're going to stop the dirty old drovers and their dirty old dogs coming past our place, but they'll still drive their smelly old cows and sheep along your end of the street. The bottom end. So there!"

"Yeah!" said Harry Jitters. "All them stinking old cow plops, and them stinking old sheep poops, too. Your end stinks!" And because Minnie Mitchell was there, he gave Jack Jackman a shove.

Later, Jack told his mother, "I just stuck out my hand to stop myself falling over. I didn't mean to punch his nose."

Harry Jitters felt his nose, saw the blood on his hand, and ran bawling for his mother.

"Look what you've done!" Minnie Mitchell screamed. "You killed poor Harry!" She clouted Jack Jackman with her basket. "You did that on purpose!"

Jack's mother always told him boys don't fight with girls, so he just stuck out his tongue at Minnie, pulled down the corners of his eyes with his second fingers, pulled up the corners of his mouth with his thumbs, waggled his ears with his index fingers, and growled, "Unga-Yunga!", deep in his throat.

Minnie Mitchell screamed louder and threw her basket in the air so the bread, the paper, and the letters dropped out. "You made me do that, Jack Jackman!" Her face went ugly as she ran shrieking, "I'm telling my mother on you!"

Once before, Jack had tried pulling his face and making his "Unga-Yunga!" noise at Mrs Mitchell, but it didn't work on her. He went for his life, and hid in the pig-fern around Mr Bryce's overgrown tennis court on the corner where Whites' Road cut across Ward Street.

Jack watched Mrs Mitchell come out her gate, grab the basket Minnie had dropped, the bread, the paper, and the letters, and jump up and down. He was too far away to hear, but he could guess what Mrs Mitchell was saying, so he dropped on his knees and crawled along one of his secret tunnels between the brown fern stems.

Safe in his secret possie, Jack stuck out his head through tight-curled fronds thick with brown dust, and took another look. He could see up Ward Street one way, and down it the other way, but he still couldn't see whether one end was higher than the other. As he watched, Mrs Mitchell went inside, and Minnie Mitchell came out. Then Harry Jitters came out, holding his head well back.

Minnie waved her arms and popped back inside her gate, and so did Harry. Then Harry popped out again, and so did Minnie, and they both waved their arms. Jack thought they looked a bit like the little old man and woman who popped in and out of the tiny house on his mother's mantelpiece and showed whether it was going to rain or shine.

Harry still stood with his head tipped well back, so he must have been looking at something in the sky, Jack thought, but Minnie stood in her usual way, admiring something about herself.

Jack Jackman jumped out of the pig-fern and shouted, "Unga-Yunga!" He stuck out his tongue, wagged his head, and did his puku dance in the middle of Ward Street. He could tell Minnie was screaming by the way she stood and pointed before running inside, and Harry was bolting for his gate, head still tipped well back.

Jack yelled, "Unga-Yunga!" again and trotted home, feeling pleased with himself.

"I thought I told you not to play in that dirty old fern!" his mother said.

Astonished, Jack asked, "How did you know I was play- ing in the fern?", but his mother just smiled to herself.

"I've got eyes that can see through doors what you're doing," she said. "I've got ears that can hear what you're going to say before you've even said it. And I've got a nose that can sniff you and tell what you've been up to! Don't you go thinking you've got any secrets from me, Jack Jackman!"

Even though he had no secrets from his mother, even though she made him stand out on the back step and brush himself all over before she let him inside, it was good to be home. The only trouble was that Jack still didn't know whether one end of Ward Street was higher than the other, nor which was up and which was down.

Chapter Four

Which Way the Water Runs,
Why Eating Smarter Pills Didn't Do
Harry Jitters Any Good, and
Giving You Something to Think About
With the Back of My Hand.

IT RAINED THAT AFTERNOON, and Jack looked at the puddles. The water lay in them and didn't run up the street; nor did it run down the street. Jack thought of what Harry Jitters had said about it and whispered, "Unga-Yunga!" quietly, in case his mother heard. She mightn't like it any more than Mrs Mitchell.

As it went on raining, the puddles joined along both sides because the road was lower there. It rained on and on, and Jack noticed the puddles didn't just join up and get longer: they got deeper and spread towards the middle of the road.

"If this is the bottom end of Ward Street," Jack said aloud, "the water would run here from the other end. But it doesn't run anywhere. It just gets deeper and spreads. Strike a light! Harry Jitters doesn't know what he's talking about."

To prove it, Jack waded through the deeper parts of

the puddles along both sides of the road, and ran through the shallower parts where the puddles were spreading towards the middle. He tried kicking the water with his right foot, which made it shoot up in sheets. Then he tried kicking it with his left foot, but that didn't work as well.

"Maybe that's because I'm right-handed," Jack said to himself. "I must be right-footed, too." That made him wonder if he was also right-eyed. So he tried closing his left eye, standing on his left foot, pointing with his right hand at Harry Jitters's end of Ward Street, and kicking with his right foot, all at once. It made a good splash.

Then he ran through the puddles again. He galloped through the shallow parts, but he had to slow down and wade through the deep parts. He stood on his right foot, pointed with his left hand, closed his right eye, and kicked with his left foot — all at the same time. It didn't make much of a splash, so he tried kicking with both feet at once and sat down in the puddle.

Few cars or lorries came along Ward Street, so it was just a dirt road without any metal. If Jack's friends Andy the Drover and Old Drumble had driven cattle along it, there were cow plops all over the place. If they'd driven sheep, there were thousands of little black bits of sheep dung like currants. Jack Jackman had once got Harry Jitters to eat a handful by telling him they were Smarter Pills. It was a story he'd heard his father tell Mr Murdoch, the carrier.

"You eat enough of them, and they'll make you smarter," Jack told Harry and pretended to swallow a handful himself.

Harry picked up a few, swallowed them, and looked thoughtful. "I don't feel any different," he complained.

"You've got to eat a decent handful for them to work." Jack pretended to eat some more, and Harry had another go at them.

"I don't think they're Smarter Pills at all. I think they're just sheep muck!" said Harry.

"Now you're getting smarter!" Jack told him.

When he tried the Smarter Pills on Minnie Mitchell, she ran and told her mother. That was the time Jack tried pulling a face and saying "Unga-Yunga!" to Mrs Mitchell. And, soon after that, Mrs Dainty, from up the street past the hall, told Jack he was a dirty-minded little boy who would come to no good.

Every now and again, on Ward Street, there'd be the round balls of dung where Andy the Drover had led his horse, following the mobs. The dust, the plops, the dung, and the muck turned to liquid mud when it rained. Where Andy and Old Drumble had driven the last mob of cattle through, a week or so before, Jack could see the dirt poached with tracks, each now a little puddle of water.

Tramping and splashing along, putting his feet in their tracks, mooing, and shaking his head from side to side, swinging his horns, and swishing his tail, Jack tried being a cattle beast. When he stamped, the muddy water shot up between his toes. From under his heels, it shot right up the back of his knees. If he stamped really hard, the muddy water shot up the legs of his shorts and felt funny, so he did that again. Again and again.

He was mooing, stamping, shaking his horns, and shooting the water right up the legs of his shorts, and wondering if he could get it to go so high that it would come out the neck of his shirt, when somebody swung him off his feet, ran him through his gate, inside the wash-house, stripped off his wet clothes, threw them to soak in one of the tubs, and told him to put on the dry clothes she had ready.

"And if I catch you thinking you're a bull, mooing and stamping in those puddles again, my boy, I'll give you something to moo about with the back of my hand," his mother told him. "The idea! As if I haven't enough to keep me busy, without having to soak your muddy clothes as well."

Chapter Five

The Silly Sort of Question Your Father Likes, Why Jack Stood on a Box and Nodded and Winked and Clicked, and Getting a Dub Home.

WARM IN DRY CLOTHES, Jack stood at the window. It had stopped raining and, because Waharoa had free-draining sand under the rich black soil on top, the puddles were already shrinking. Jack watched them getting smaller and said to his mother, "It's a shame to waste them."

"You keep out of those puddles," said his mother, "or I'll give you waste . . . "

"Mum," said Jack. "If this is the top end of Ward Street, why doesn't all the water run down the other end? If the other end's the bottom end."

"As if it's not enough that I've got all this extra work you've made for me: traipsing water and mud all through the house! Do you think I've got time to worry about which way the water runs along Ward Street, and which end's the bottom and which is the top? Ask your father, when he comes home. It's just the silly sort of question he likes."

While Jack waited for his father to come home, he

looked out the window again to see if the puddles ran away. As far as he could see, they just lay there, getting smaller. Already, the middle of the road was clear of water when Mr Kennedy drove past in his flash Plymouth and gave Jack a nod. Mr Kennedy's car had mud splashed up the side, so he must have come through some pretty big puddles up the Matamata road, Jack thought, as he nodded back.

But Jack's nod wasn't the sort of nod Mr Kennedy had given him. When his father and Mr Kennedy and all the other men nodded, the top of their heads went one way, and their chins swung the other way. Sometimes, just as they finished the nod, they winked one eye, and sometimes they screwed up the corner of their mouths and made a click. Andy the Drover did it all the time.

Jack had practised it in the bathroom mirror, but he couldn't seem to get it right. When he did the nod, he forgot to close one eye, or his head went up and down instead of sideways. He went out to the wash-house now, stood on a box so he could look in the mirror over the hand basin, and nodded at himself. His eye didn't close, and his chin didn't seem to swing to one side, not the way Andy's did. And he couldn't get the click right. It didn't sound like "Click!", it didn't come at the right time, and he thought he looked silly, so he poked out his tongue, tried to say, "Unga-Yunga!" to it, and bit it.

He tried several more times and was just thinking

he'd got it right, nodding his head, winking one eye, and clicking his tongue against the roof of his mouth, when his mother's voice said, "What on earth are you up to now? Shaking your head, blinking into the mirror, and making that noise. Get off that box at once, and find yourself something useful to do.

"Anyway, what are you doing inside, getting under my feet and upsetting my house? Why aren't you outside, running around and making the most of it while the rain's stopped?"

Jack didn't remind his mother that she'd ordered him to keep inside out of the puddles and mud. He shot out the door before she changed her mind again, galloped through the water that was left, and made channels in the mud with his heel so one puddle could run into the next along the side of the road and help him make up his mind which end of Ward Street was up and which was down. Away down the other end of Ward Street, Harry Jitters was doing the same thing, but it was too far for Jack to see whether he was still holding his head well back.

Jack found he could get the water to run from one puddle into another, all right, but sometimes it emptied out of a puddle towards his end of Ward Street, and sometimes it emptied towards the other end. He was still trying to work out which was the top and which was the bottom when he heard the voice he'd been waiting for.

"You'll catch it from your mother, splashing around

in the mud, getting your clothes wet. Here, jump up and I'll give you a dub home."

Jack put one foot on top of his father's boot on the pedal, climbed on the bar, rang the bell, and asked, "Dad, which is the top end of Ward Street?"

His father whistled. "Now that's an interesting question!" Jack thought of what his mother had said and grinned over the handlebars at the front mudguard. "We call this the top end, because we live up here," said his father. "Down where Harry Jitters lives, that's the other end to us, so we call it the bottom end."

"But Harry reckons his is the top end and ours is the bottom end."

"That's how it looks to him," said Jack's father. "But from up our end, he's down the bottom end. We go down to his end, but he comes up to our end.

"When I think of it," he told Jack, "I have to pedal to get up to our end, from down Harry's end. But I have to pedal to get down his end from up our end as well. You realise what that means?"

"Does it mean that Ward Street goes down in the middle?"

"Maybe." Jack felt his father shake his head as he pedalled in their gate, around the back of the house, and said, "I suppose you realise it could mean that Ward Street's flat."

Chapter Six

Why They Dug the Drains With a Fall in Them,
Why You Don't Want to Think About
Making a Click When You Nod, and
How Jack Knew His Mother
Was Having Him On.

JACK WASN'T SURE that he wanted Ward Street to be flat. He rang the bell again and said, "I thought if the puddles ran away down the street to Harry's end, that would make our end the top end."

"And did they?"

"They just ran into each other and soaked away." With his big toe, Jack felt for his father's boot, curved his foot to fit it, and slipped off the bar.

"We're on pretty free-draining soil, you know. And there's the big drains all round Waharoa for the water to soak into. This district was all swamp in the old days, so they dug the drains and dried it out to turn it into farms, but the water still runs in the drains okay, because they were dug with a fall in them." His father leaned his bike against the shed.

"What's a fall?"

"They dug the drains deeper at one end than the other,

with a fall, a slope, so the water runs along them. They all run into the creek that comes down through the Domain and winds through Mr Weeks's bush and Mr Hawe's, then out through Wardville and into the Waihou River downstream of the Gordon bridge."

"Has the Waihou got a fall in it?"

"That's why it runs downstream. And up near Okoroire, it's got waterfalls in it as well!"

Jack tried to follow the drains and creeks in his mind. It was like making a map inside his head, he thought. At the same time, he tried to think about falling all the way from Ward Street into the Waihou River, until he felt dizzy.

"Has that boy been playing in the puddles again? Just look at the state of him! He's had one change already this afternoon. Oh, what's the use of trying to keep him presentable when he goes straight out and gets covered in mud again?"

"It's my fault, dear," said Mr Jackman. "I rode through a puddle, and the mud and water shot up all over him. Still he saved me getting it all over my trousers." He nodded at Jack, that peculiar shake of his head. The top of his head went one way, his chin went the other, one eye winked, his mouth screwed up and the corner of his mouth went "Click!"

Jack tried to do it back, but his wink went wrong, both eyes closed, and he didn't get a click.

His father looked solemn. "People see things differently," he told Jack. "From Harry's place, we look down the bottom end, and from our place, he looks down the bottom end. It depends where you're looking from."

"I thought I made it perfectly clear," Jack's mum told them both. "Ours is the top end of Ward Street. Now wash your hands and get yourselves ready for your tea, the pair of you."

"People see things differently," Jack said to himself as he washed the mud off his legs and feet under the outside tap. He was nodding to himself and winking one eye when his mother called, "Will you stop wasting that water? The rain just filled the tanks, but they'll be half empty by the time you've finished. Your tea's on the table, and your father's waiting to start his. Now come inside at once, or everything'll be cold. I don't know, what's the point of going to all that trouble, heating the plates, when nobody can be bothered getting to the table on time?"

"Dad?" said Jack, feeling the backs of his legs wet against the chair. "You know when you nod, how the top of your head sort of goes this way, and your chin goes that way, and you wink, and you screw up that corner of your mouth, and you make a click?"

His father took a forkful of mashed potato, looked at Jack, and nodded straight up and down.

"Well, do you make the click with the corner of your mouth, or do you make it with your tongue?"

Jack's dad nodded so the left top of his head went one way, his chin went the other, his left eye winked, and the right side of his mouth screwed up and went "Click!"

"I think I clicked with the corner of my mouth," he said. "Hold on, I'll just swallow this mouthful of mashed potato and try it again." He tried, but no click came this time. "It's not the sort of thing you want to think about doing."

Jack stared.

"Think about it and it doesn't work."

"I had trouble, too!" Jack said. "I can't get my eye to wink, and the click won't come. I tried it with my tongue and with the corner of my mouth, but it didn't work either way."

"I'll try nodding it to the other side," said his father. He laid down his knife and fork and nodded the top of his head to the right and his chin to the left, and the left corner of his mouth screwed up and a click came out of it. A good one. "I don't think I used my tongue at all," he said. "Besides, there wasn't any mashed potato to get in the way."

Jack tried to copy him. They tried nodding this way, and they tried nodding that way; and they both had trouble remembering to wink their eyes and make the clicks because they were thinking about it. Jack's dad was better at it, but even he got mixed up sometimes, and Jack didn't seem able to get the wink right at all.

Not if he clicked. And he couldn't get the click going if he winked.

They were clicking and winking and nodding when Jack's mum turned from the stove.

"I thought so!" she said. "Pulling faces and winking at each other behind my back. That's all the gratitude I get for spending the afternoon bent over a hot stove getting tea ready for the pair of you. All you can think to do is to make a mockery of me!" She slammed her plate down on the table, slumped into her chair, threw her apron over her head, and burst into tears.

"Mum!" Jack shouted as he leapt up. "We weren't making a mockery out of you! Honest!" But he sat down again when he saw his mother grinning under her apron. She was having him on.

"Now get on with your tea, and we'll have no more of this clicking and winking and nodding. As for you, you'd think a grown man would know better than to go teaching the boy a lot of silly nonsense when he should be eating his tea." Without stopping for breath, his mother said, "Next time Andy the Drover comes through, why don't you ask him to teach you how to nod and wink and click the corner of your mouth? He's better at such things than your father. He's been doing it twice as long.

"Now, hurry up and finish your greens, I've got a nice golden syrup pudding for you. And after that I'll make your father a cup of tea and you can give me a hand to get the dishes done, and then it'll be time for you to get to bed. I wonder when Andy will be along? He promised to drop in a cutting off Mrs Charlie Ryan's camellia, her white one."

"If Andy comes," Jack said, "can I help him drive the sheep?"

"Drive the sheep?"

"Oh!" Jack whined with his voice going up. He thought of finishing with a click, but stopped just in time.

"What will the boy be asking next?"

"Just down the other end of Ward Street?"

"We'll see," said Jack's mother. "Mind you, I'm not promising anything."

Chapter Seven

Why Jack Watched to See Andy
Take Off His Hat, Just As Far As the
Bottom of the Street and Not a Step Further,
and What Reminded Jack of the
Governor-General's Plumed Hat.

ANDY THE DROVER turned up on Tuesday morning, his
mob of sheep left over the other side of the hall corner,
where there was never any traffic and they had a bit of
grass.

"Where's Old Drumble?" asked Jack.

"Holding them." Andy nodded back past the hall, and
Jack saw Old Drumble standing, daring the sheep to move
a foot nearer the corner. "Old Nell and Young Nugget,
they're back the other end of the mob," said Andy.

He was taking his reins, passing the bight through the
fence wires, up and over the top of a post. Nosy, his old
horse, was smart at opening gates. She'd never worked
out how to get her reins off the fence yet, but set about
it now, as Andy reached inside the split sack — what he
called a pikau — over Nosy's back, behind the saddle.

"What would Nosy do if she got her reins undone?"
Jack asked.

"Mooch along the fence and munch the heads off your mother's flowers. She wouldn't like that — I mean your mother — I'd never hear the end of it. Or she might wander back and have a word with Old Drumble. She wouldn't go far," said Andy. "Those two stick together. They like each other's company." He pulled out a carefully packed sugarbag from inside the pikau.

Andy's voice was dry and creaky, from walking and riding in the dust behind a thousand mobs of sheep and cattle. His face was dry and creaky, too, with grooves worn by the wind and the rain, the sun, the frosts, the hot days and the cold days, springs and autumns, winters and summers through which he'd driven stock up and down, across and around the North Island.

He slept on the ground, in a tent, in huts, under trees, in haystacks, in scrub, under bridges, in barns and sheds, in long grass, in short grass, on stones, on rocks, on logs, on sand, on thistles, on branches, on piles of leaves. "You name it, Jack, and I reckon I've slept on it," Andy always said, and he walked with a slight crouch, as if his back hurt.

Andy had a white scar on one arm where a scared horse had bitten him. He had a healed red tear in the right corner of his mouth where a cattle beast had caught its horn and ripped open his cheek. One of his fingers was bent where he had cut a tendon while dog-tuckering a sheep. His face and hands and arms and legs were a tangle of lines, grooves, and scars, each with its story.

He wore a broad-brimmed hat against the rain and the sun. He wore a long oilskin coat in the wet, and rolled it in front of his saddle in the dry. Both his hat and his oilskins were dusty, lined, and grooved like his face and hands, and they were dry and creaky, too.

He wore an old suit jacket that had once been black, but now was the colour of the roads he'd walked and ridden. Under his jacket he wore a waistcoat with umpteen pockets. It was the colour of the roads, like his saddle-tweed trousers and his hobnailed boots, which he called his Bill Masseys. They looked dry and creaked today because the road was dusty.

Jack liked the look of Andy's face, his hands and arms, his clothes, and his boots. He liked the dry, creaky sound of his voice. He liked his stories. Most of all, he liked Andy's rich smell: the smell of cows and sheep and horses and dogs, smoke and dust, the smell of the drover, the smell of the road. It made Jack think of places he hadn't seen, of places he wanted to see, places he didn't even know about. When Andy mentioned the names of roads and rivers and districts far away from Waharoa, Jack listened and thought the words were like music, rare and strange.

"Some day, I'm going to see all those places you talk about," he'd say to Andy the Drover.

"You'll have a cup of tea?" Jack's mother called from

the door. "Don't worry about your boots." She'd filled the teapot and flung down a row of sacks so Andy could tramp inside and sit at the table without his hobnails taking the polish off the lino.

Jack waited to see Andy take off his hat. His grooved and lined face was as brown as the back of his hands but, when he took off his old, dry, creaky hat, his skull from above his eyes to the back of his head was a startling colour, muddy white like a boiled suet pudding. Andy put his hat on the floor under his chair, winked at Jack's stare, asked after his father, emptied a cup of tea, and opened the sugarbag.

As Jack's mother refilled his cup, Andy said, "There's the last of Mrs Jenkins's asparagus, and she won't be at Institute this coming Wednesday because she's going over to Cambridge with her sister, Biddy, to see their cousin, Ethel, the one who's moving down Gisborne way to be near her parents. They must be getting on a bit."

"Going all that way!" said Jack's mother. "It might as well be the other side of the world, for all Mrs Jenkins will see of her now."

"It's where she grew up. There's a few chops to keep you going," said Andy, dumping a brown paper parcel on the table, "and there's the comfrey root Mrs Burns said she'd let you have. 'Keep it watered,' she said, 'it'll take off, no trouble, and it doesn't mind a bit of shade.'

She says just to scrape a bit of the root when you want a poultice; use the brown outside as well as the lighter-coloured inside. You can put it on hot or cold. Nothing to touch it for drawing a boil or a stone-bruise, so she reckons.

"Oh, I nearly forgot, there's a setting of eggs in that tin — Mrs McKenzie said you've got a clucky chook. They're Rhode Island Reds, good layers and sensible chooks to have around. They lay a nice brown egg.

"And here," Andy said, "that camellia cutting Mrs Ryan's been promising you for ages." He took a clay pot from the bottom of the sugarbag.

"That's not a cutting — she's struck it for me! Oh, I must let her have the jasmine she's been wanting." Jack's mother nodded. "I'll give you a loaf of bread, if you wouldn't mind dropping it in to Mrs Kennedy. You'll be passing her place. And there's a jar of marmalade for yourself, and one for Mrs Feak. You can take a tin of ginger-nuts when you go, and I wonder if you've got room for a cake for old Mrs Gray? She does like a bit of fruit cake, and she's not up to making them for herself these days. Her poor old hands, it's the rheumatism, you know."

Andy nodded and drank his tea. He and Mum talked about how Mr Gaunt's front paddock was closed up for hay, and how it had come on since that rain last week, how Arnolds' big macrocarpa hedge up the Matamata road was needing clipping or it'd get out of hand, and how Eileen MacLean was coming back to take a job teaching at Hinuera School. Jack listened as the messages and gossip went to and fro.

Then Andy was on his feet, fishing up his hat from under his chair, hiding his astonishing skull, carefully stowing the reloaded sugarbag in Nosy's pikau, flipping his reins off the fence, whistling and waving to Old Drumble, Old Nell, and Young Nugget. Jack heard some barking and, Old Drumble leading, the sheep came pouring across the Turangaomoana Road and along Ward Street.

"Can I give Andy and Old Drumble a hand, Mum?" Jack asked. "Just as far as the other end of the street? You promised, Mum!"

"I never promised a thing!" Jack's mother looked at his face. "Oh, I suppose so. But just as far as the bottom of the street," she said, "and not a step further. You make sure you stop there, and come home at once."

Old Drumble trotted over, nosed the back of Jack's hand, and trotted back to his place at the head of the mob. Reins hooked over his arm, Andy waited and fell in behind, stick in his hand. Jack walked beside him. Young Nugget rushed from one side of the road to the other. Old Nell took it more quietly. And up the front, over the backs of the sheep, a black and white tail waved high in the air.

The back of his hand still wet from Old Drumble's nose, Jack looked at the tail and grinned. It reminded him of the feathers on the governor-general's plumed hat, in the photo in the *Weekly News*.

Chapter Eight

How Old Drumble Was a Handy Dog and Carried a Map of the North Island in His Head, How He Won Andy the Bet, and Why Jack Barked at the Outside Tap.

JACK TRIED TO LOOK as if his face was all leathery, dusty creases; he tried to sound creaky when he walked; and he tried to take steps the same length as Andy's. When Andy whistled, Jack pursed up his lips and tried to whistle, too. When Andy waved a signal to the dogs, Jack wagged his hand, too, but behind his back.

Old Drumble paused at the corner of Whites' Road, made sure there was nothing coming, and led the mob on down Ward Street.

"That Old Drumble, he's what you call a handy dog." Andy licked a crumb of ginger-nut off his moustache. "He can hustle them along with a bark like a huntaway, and he can head, and work them silently 'cause he's got a bit of strong-eye in him, too. You can see the border collie in his head and his tail, and the huntaway in the length of leg."

Jack nodded and said he could see the border collie in Old Drumble's head and tail, and the huntaway in the length of leg.

"He's as good on cattle as he is on sheep. He'll split a mob to let a car through, and he'll lead all day and never make a mistake. See how he's dropped back to one side because he spotted that somebody's left their gate open? You'd think folk who live on a stock route would have more sense. You watch, and you'll see Old Nell move up into the gateway, and he'll take the lead again.

"There he goes. He knows there could be trouble at the church corner, turning them out on to the main road."

"How does Old Drumble know?" Jack asked, but Andy just grinned and wiped his moustache with the back of his hand.

"Old Drumble knows every corner of every road, every gateway, every fence, and every farm in about six provinces, I reckon. It's like he carries a map of the North Island inside his head." Andy shook his own head in wonder.

"Once for a bet, y'know, I give him six sheep and says to him, 'Take these sheep to Waharoa.' We were just this side of Rotorua, coming past Ngongotaha Mountain, and I've got to see a cocky, around the lake, about a mob of cattle beasts he wants brought up from Opotiki. At the turn-off for the Mamakus, I says, 'Old Drumble, you take these here six ewes to Waharoa, and put them into the school horse paddock. I'll be along in a day or two.'

"And, y'know, Jack, when I gets to Waharoa four or five days later, them six ewes are in the school horse paddock, and Old Drumble's lying across the gateway so they can't get out. He's smart enough to open the gate, Old Drumble, but he couldn't figure out how to shove it closed again. Of course, that gate gets a bit heavy from time to time, even for a man.

"The headmaster, Mr Strap, he told me that Old Drumble rounded up them six ewes at the same time each evening, trotted them down the Turangaomoana road as far as the Domain corner, and put them down the bank of the creek under the bridge, to water them. Then back he brings them to the horse paddock, turns them in for the night, and lies down across the gate-way again."

"Did you win your bet?"

"Did I what?" said Andy. "Five bob that bet won me off young Tom Cookson, and five bob each off his mates, Mick Ruruhi and Russ Tulloch. Fifteen bob all told. They won't be in a hurry to go laying bets against Old Drumble again, more's the pity."

"What did Old Drumble do for tucker himself?"

"I give him a few bob," Andy said, "when I started him off from Ngongotaha. Each morning, once the ewes were feeding quietly, Old Drumble nicked across the track to Mrs Besant's bakery and bought himself a mince pie. It only took him a couple of minutes, and he'd be back sitting on top of the gatepost, blowing on his pie and chewing it, and keeping an eye on his little flock. He's very fond of a hot mince pie, Old Drumble."

"Didn't he get thirsty?"

"Course he did. A dog drinks a lot more than a sheep. But he knew how to turn on the school drinking fountain, when he wanted a drink. It only took him a few seconds to lap up a gutsful, and the sheep didn't have time to notice he'd been gone."

"Hello, Jack!"

Jack glanced and saw Harry Jitters and Minnie Mitchell waving from behind their gates. He looked straight ahead, as if he'd never seen them before, and strode out beside Andy, his face all creased and leathery, as if he'd been droving all his life. For a moment he thought of whistling Young Nugget and giving him an order.

"One thing you never do, you never give orders to another man's dogs," said Andy. "Here's the bottom of the street, and see how Old Drumble's heading for the church corner? He'll take a mosey round, make sure the main road's clear of traffic, then lead the mob out and turn them right. This is as far as you come, Jack."

"Mum wouldn't mind me going to the church corner, just to see Old Drumble lead them out on to the main road," Jack said, but Andy grinned and shook his head.

"Maybe next time, but you're not getting me into hot

water, young fellow-me-lad. Your mum said the bottom of the street and not a step further. Thank her for the cup of tea, it's always a real life-saver, and tell her I said them ginger-nuts of hers are in a class of their own!"

Jack stood at the bottom of Ward Street and watched them go down to the church corner and disappear. He was too far away to see how Old Drumble managed to turn the mob right. Slowly, Jack turned himself around; slowly, he took a couple of steps homeward; then something perked him up so, instead of dragging his feet, he strutted.

Harry Jitters was coming out of his gate, and Minnie Mitchell was coming out of hers. As their mouths opened, Jack whistled, not a high, loud whistle like Andy's, but still a whistle. He pointed to the side of the road, and an invisible handy dog ran to turn back several ewes. Jack whistled again, so the invisible dog barked noisily and drove them straight on up Ward Street.

"Better close your gates, unless you want sheep all through your garden!" Jack didn't look at Minnie and Harry, but heard their gates slam shut.

"Townies!" Dancing between sheep muck like black currants scattered all over the road, whistling and waving and working his dogs. Jack drove his mob all the way back home — to the top end of Ward Street — and left them across by the hall, where they had something to eat, and his handy dog would hold them.

"Next time Andy brings a mob through, he says I can watch Old Drumble put them round the church corner and turn them right on to the main road," Jack told his mother. "And the cup of tea was a life-saver, and I was to tell you he said your ginger-nuts are in a class of their own. Can I go down the church corner next time? Mum? Can I go down the church corner next time, Mum? Andy said I could. Mum?"

"Just look at those feet. You wash them under the outside tap before you even think of taking a step on my clean lino. This instant!"

"Oh, Mum!"

"Will you get out of my kitchen with your never-ending chatter and questions? And smart about it, or I'll take the broom to you. We'll see when the time comes. And once you've washed those feet, you can make yourself useful and chop me some kindling for the morning."

"Gee, thanks, Mum!" Jack said.

"I haven't said a word about the church corner. Don't go thinking just because you've been allowed to go as far as the bottom of the street this once, that you can do it again. Out you go. Out. This moment!"

His mother banged the back door behind him, but Jack grinned. He scrubbed his feet, his legs, even his knees, under the outside tap. He lapped up a gutsful of water, barked twice, and made sure he didn't leave the tap dripping. And he chopped enough kindling to last his mother the rest of the week.

His mother heard his barks, then the sound of the tomahawk. She looked out the kitchen window and smiled. "I know what you're up to, my boy!" she murmured. "Think you're one jump ahead of your mother, do you? Well, you've got another think coming."

Chapter Nine

How to Keep the Flies Off Smoked Trout,
Why Old Drumble Didn't Want to be
Reminded About Fishing Without a Licence,
and Barking in the Swagger's Earhole.

Next time Andy the Drover came through Ward
Street, it was from the northern end, and he was riding
Nosy and running a Jersey bull up to the Matamata
saleyards. The bull had a couple of steers for company,
and Old Drumble, Old Nell, and Young Nugget kept
them on the trot along Ward Street. Nobody wanted
any trouble from a Jersey bull, so voices yelled from
backyard to backyard, "There's a bull coming! Is your
front gate closed? Peter, run and close Mrs Harris's
gate." Harry Jitters and Minnie Mitchell hid as the bull
rolled by.

Jack Jackman was in the bamboo patch along the road,
cutting himself a pea shooter, so he didn't even know
Andy had come through. His mother said she'd caught a
glimpse of them, that was all.

"He'll let them have a blow when he gets them past the
last houses and on to the stock road up to Matamata.

"I'm surprised you didn't hear them: what with Andy

cracking his whip, and his dogs barking, they made a hullabaloo, enough to raise the dead. Just as well, too, because I saw Mrs Dainty bolt back in her gate till they'd gone past. She's been terrified of bulls ever since Mr Lewis's broke through her fence, knocked down her clothes-line, and ran halfway out to the Kaimais with her nightie flapping on its horns."

It was several days before Andy's stained old hat came bobbing past the kitchen window. Jack's mother was expecting him and had the teapot filled, the plateful of ginger-nuts on the table, and the cups, the milk, and the sugar set out and waiting before he could poke his head in the back door.

Jack wanted to run to where the mob was feeding, past the hall, and have a word with Old Drumble, but he tore out, patted Nosy, waved to Old Drumble, and tore back inside again so he wouldn't miss anything. Besides, he had something he wanted to remind his mother about.

In the kitchen, Andy was taking a cylindrical bundle of tightly tied tea-tree brush out of his sugarbag, and undoing it. The bundle unrolled, opened, and there — lying in a green bed of watercress — was a smoked rainbow trout which had been kept airy and fresh, yet protected from flies by the mesh of twigs and tiny leaves.

Jack sniffed at the rich smell of tea-tree and smoked trout and felt his mouth fill with dribble.

"From Mrs Henry," said Andy, and drank his tea. "Her husband caught a couple of good fish away up in the head of that little stream, the Waimakariri, the other side of Tirau.

"It was all I could do not to eat it, walking along and sniffing the smell of smoked trout," he told Jack. "And Old Drumble, he kept dropping back and glancing up at the pikau. He knew what was in it."

"Does Old Drumble like trout?"

"Like trout? If he had his way, he'd spend all day fishing for them, all night smoking them, and all the next day eating them.

"Of course, he's not a dry fly man, Old Drumble. I've told him there's more satisfaction fishing upstream, but there's no talking to the old coot when he's got a rod in his hand. He's so keen to catch a fish and smoke it, he doesn't hear a word you say. Besides, he reckons he gets more fun out of a wet fly, and I've got to admit, he catches more fish than I do."

"Has he got a rod?" Jack asked.

"An old split cane rod of mine that I give him for a birthday present," said Andy. "And I make sure he buys a licence each year. He got caught fishing without one, when he was just a pup, and the ranger took him to court, dragged him up in front of the beak. His lawyer pleaded his youthfulness, but the magistrate said there was too much poaching going on, and Young Drumble had to cough up thirty bob."

"Did he pay the fine?"

"Where was a young dog going to get thirty bob from? Young Drumble didn't have two pennies to rub together, so the magistrate put him in the hinaki for a week. It taught him a lesson he's never forgotten. Old Drumble doesn't like being reminded of his time as a gaolbird, so I wouldn't go saying anything about it to him, not if I was you, Jack."

Mrs Jackman turned from hanging the smoked trout from a cuphook in the safe. "That's such a lovely fish, Andy! We'll have it for our tea, with a fresh lettuce out of the garden. When you're coming back through Waharoa, I'll give you some marmalade for Mrs Henry."

Jack said nothing about Old Drumble's fishing, because he knew his mother wouldn't like it, specially not the bit about him going to gaol. He listened to Andy and Mum talking about how Mr Gaunt's hay was doing, and how good the Arnolds' big macrocarpa hedge was looking.

"Time was," Andy said, "when every farm in the province had one along their road frontage. They used to say a macrocarpa hedge needs a whole family of boys to keep it in shape. That's why a lot of them got out of hand during the Great War. Then families got smaller, and there weren't the boys to do the clipping, so the cockies started pulling them out. Let a macrocarpa hedge get away on you, and you can't cut it back without getting those dead bits here and there that spoil the look.

"Mrs Charlie Ryan says to tell you her big hydrangea just up and died without warning — I think she'd like a cutting off that blue one of yours; and she said that Eileen MacLean's getting on fine at Hinuera School. She straightened out those Tulloch scamps her first week, and hasn't had a peep out of them since."

As Andy loaded his sugarbag with bread and cakes and biscuits, and a jar of marmalade for old Mrs Gray, Jack said to his mother, "Can I go down to the church corner with Andy?"

"What's this?"

"You promised, Mum!"

"I did nothing of the sort!"

"Aw!"

"Oh, well, I suppose you can go. But just as far as the church corner, and not a step further. No going out on the main road. And straight home. No stopping to play down the other end of Ward Street. You make sure you send him straight home, Andy."

Before his mother had finished, before Andy could hide his amazing skull under his hat, Jack was streaking across the hall corner to help Old Drumble lead the sheep over the Turangaomoana road and down Ward Street.

As he fell to the back of the mob and walked beside

Andy and Nosy, Jack said, "I didn't say anything to Old Drumble about being a gaolbird." Andy nodded.

"It must be a long time ago now," said Jack. "Do you think he still remembers?"

"I'll tell you what," said Andy, "that dog's got a better memory than most people."

"Really?"

Andy nodded. "Old Drumble's got what you call a photographic memory. He could have had a career as a detective. Never forgets a face.

"Years ago, I was taking a mob of steers through the back road, out Okauia, taking them to Old Man Parson's place. Hot day, dry dirt road: a man was eating dust. Just before the bridge, Nosy shies a bit, to let me know there's something going on, and I looks down and sees this swagger lying back with his bare feet in the creek: smoke drifting up from the embers where he's boiled his billy, hat pulled over his face, having forty winks. I looks at the cool water and thinks to myself: 'I wouldn't mind swapping places with you, mate,' but just then Old Drumble comes padding up beside me and tries to catch me eye.

"I don't take any notice of Old Drumble, just watch that none of them cattle try to shoot off down the side of the bridge — it's a favourite trick of theirs. They know you've got to send a dog after them, then they get themselves penned into a corner, and you finish up going down yourself and working them out and up on to the road again. And then, nine times out of ten, they take off up the road the way you've just come, and you've got to send somebody to turn them back.

"Well, Old Drumble gives a bit of a whine. Next thing he jumps down, takes the swagger by the shoulder, gives him a good shake, and wakes him with a bark fair in the earhole. It must have been enough to wake the dead."

"Enough to wake the dead," Jack thought to himself and wondered what on earth Andy meant.

Chapter Ten

How Old Drumble Recognised Tuppenny Bill,
Why Minnie Told Harry He Was Silly, and How
Jack's Mother Could See Him Through the
Door and Tell What He Was Thinking.

"Was the swagger dead?" asked Jack. "Is that why Old
Drumble barked in his earhole?"

Andy shook his head. "Not on your Nelly! He was
just out the monk, having a moe, but he comes to pretty
smartly with that thundering bark in his ear.

"He reaches out for his hat that Old Drumble had sent
flying with a wag of his tail, jumps to his feet, and looks
straight up into me eyes where a man's standing on the
sill of the bridge, looking down at him.

"'Andy!' the swagger calls up to me. 'It's been a few
years since I seen you, and I reckon your old dog knows
me better than you do.'

"It's only then that I recognise him — Old Tuppenny Bill
who used to do a bit of post-splitting over Putaruru way.

"'G'day, Tuppenny!' I says to him, and he says again,
'You wouldn't have known me but for Old Drumble.'

"Anyway," Andy said to Jack, "Tuppenny Bill puts his
hat back on, kicks his fire together and swings the billy.

The cattle graze along the side of the road, and we have a brew and yarn about old times.

"'Last time I heard of you,' I says to Tuppenny Bill, 'somebody told me you'd had a run-in with the Rawleighs Man up Putaruru.'

"'It's true,' says Tuppenny Bill. "'Me old woman give me a hiding, and run away with the Rawleighs Man. I was that pleased to see the back of her, and I hadn't had so much as a day off from the post-splitting for years, so I thought of going on the swag. Just for a change, like. It's been a bit of all right, too.

"'Mind you,' Old Tuppenny says to me, 'there hasn't been much rain this season, so a man's slept pretty comfy. It's not a bad life, you know, on the swag!'

"'Not a bad life on the swag!'" Andy repeated to Jack. "'Sleeping comfy!' I knew Tuppenny Bill was on the swag because he didn't have any work. He'd lost his contract post-splitting 'cause he hit the turps when his wife ran off, but he wasn't going to say so. A man's got his pride after all.

"Moving round the country as I do, I'd heard of a job going on an orchard near Gate Pa, over at Tauranga, and I put old Tuppenny Bill on to it.

"He hoofed it over the Kaimais, got the job, and he's been there ever since; matter of fact, he finished up marrying the widow who owned the orchard. So he come out of it all right."

"What about his first wife, the one who ran away with the Rawleighs Man?"

"Oh, that wasn't a proper marriage. You know, they just jumped the broomstick."

"Jumped the broomstick?" Jack thought to himself, but Andy was still talking.

"Yes, Old Tuppenny Bill's a rich man today and, you know, he'd still be on the swag, if it hadn't been for Old Drumble and his photographic memory."

"There's just one thing," said Jack.

"What's that?"

"Tuppenny Bill's hat," said Jack. "He'd pulled it over his face as he lay there with his feet in the creek, having a snooze under the bridge. How could Old Drumble tell who it was when the hat was covering his face?"

Andy nodded. "When I said Old Drumble never forgets a face, I should have reminded you he's an eye dog, one of the strongest eyes in the business. He must've looked straight through Tuppenny Bill's hat, while he was lying on the bank of the creek, seen his face, and recognised it at once."

"Old Drumble sounds like Mum!" said Jack. "She only has to look at me to know whether I'm telling the truth or not. She can see what I'm up to through a closed door. And she knows what I'm going to say before I've even finished thinking about it. She must have a strong eye, too."

"I suppose you could say your mother's got a strong eye," Andy agreed, "but I don't know that I'd go saying it to her face. It's a funny thing, Jack, but a lot of women don't like being compared to a dog."

"I wouldn't mind being compared to Old Drumble."

"Me neither," said Andy. "But you'll find the women-folk different. They don't think the same way as a man. You ask your father.

"Here's the church corner. Watch, and you'll see how Old Drumble makes sure there's nothing coming either way, then leads them out on the main road, and turns them north."

Jack watched Old Drumble hold the mob, look both ways and wait till a milk lorry from the dairy factory drove past, then lead the mob on to the main road. Just how he told them to start off, Jack couldn't see, but the sheep did exactly what Old Drumble wanted.

Andy followed at the back, with Old Nell and Young Nugget barking and giving the stragglers a hurry-up on to the main road. Andy nodded, winked, clicked the corner of his mouth, and said, "Be seeing you, Jack!" all at the same time.

"Hooray, Andy!" Jack got that much out, and nodded back, but his head and chin tried to go to the same side, his eyes watered instead of winking, and he got no click. By the time he could see straight again, there was no sign of Old Drumble's tail, but Jack knew it was there, floating at the head of the mob. Then Andy and Nosy were disappearing round the bend towards the railway crossing, a single bark drifted back, and Jack turned and trotted for home.

Just as he strode past her place, Minnie Mitchell came out her gate, smiling, and Harry Jitters came fast out of his gate and stood near her.

"It looks funny when you wave your arms and talk to yourself," said Minnie.

"Yeah!" growled Harry.

"I'm not talking to meself," Jack told them. "I'm workin' me dogs!" He nodded, winked one eye, clicked the corner of his mouth, and signalled with one hand to his invisible dogs, who held the mob while he turned back to Minnie and Harry.

"You know Old Drumble?"

"Huh!" said Harry. "Who's Old Drumble?"

"Old Drumble's famous all over the Waikato for his astonishing memory. The police use him to nose out the worst criminals. They can try dressing up as swaggers, but Old Drumble sees through their disguise at once. The police wanted him to work for them full-time, but he said he'd rather be Andy the Drover's leading dog."

Jack shook his head. "I thought you'd have known about Old Drumble," he said to Harry. "Just about everyone else in the district does."

Harry shifted from one foot to the other and said "Gawn!"

Minnie Mitchell glanced at him. "I know who Old Drumble is," she said.

"I'll tell you what," Jack told Harry Jitters, "you might not know who Old Drumble is, but you can be sure he knows who you are. He never forgets a face, not even if you try and hide it under your hat. And he never forgets a name either."

Harry Jitters stared after Jack as he went up Ward Street. At Whites' Road, Jack waved one arm, pointed, and Harry heard him whistle.

"He looks a nut case," Harry said in a loud voice. "They ought to lock him up in the loony bin."

"You're silly!" Minnie turned her back, shook her curls, and skipped back inside her gate. Up the top end of Ward Street, Jack broke into a trot.

"You took your time coming home," his mother said. She didn't look up from the bench, where she was fitting a piece of twisted pastry around the edge of a pie dish. "I could tell what you were going to ask even before you opened the door. Can you go as far as the railway crossing and the corner of Cemetery Road next time Andy comes through? Well, the answer's no! So don't even bother asking."

Jack stared. His mother hadn't just seen through the door with her strong eye — she'd even been able to tell he was going to ask if he could go as far as the crossing and Cemetery Road corner next time. He opened his mouth, but only a sort of "Click" came out. Not the click that Andy made, but a sucking sort of click of astonishment.

"Close your mouth," his mother told him, still not looking around at him. "You look as if you're catching flies. It's not the end of the world. We'll see whether you can go as far as the corner of Cemetery Road when the time comes." She dipped a little brush in milk, and wiped it over the pastry.

"Gee, thanks, Mum! Are we having pie for lunch?"

"I didn't say you could go as far as the corner of Cemetery Road. All I said was that we'd see when the times comes."

Chapter Eleven

Why Jack's Mother Barked and Snapped
Her Teeth, How Horses Crawl Under Gates
and Have Terrible Hangovers, and
Why Harry Jitters Said He Was Not Ham Snot.

"Now, GET OUT OF MY WAY," said Jack's mother. She twiddled the twisted pastry, and pressed a spoon around the edge to make a scalloped pattern. Jack looked at the wavy edge and swallowed. He loved pastry. The pie funnel in the middle looked like a little volcano waiting to erupt.

"Out of my way, so I can open the oven door and get this pie cooked in time for your father's lunch."

"Corker, I love pie! Mum, did you know Old Drumble's got such a strong eye he can see through things? He saw through a swagger's hat once. The swagger had pulled it over his face, but Old Drumble saw through it and recognised him at once because he never forgets a face. He's got a strong eye, just like you, Mum."

"The idea! Are you comparing me with a dirty old dog?"

Jack looked nervously at the oven door and thought of the pie baking inside. "I didn't mean you look like Old

Drumble, Mum. I just meant he saw through Tuppenny Bill's hat, like you said you could see what I was up to through the door. And I thought it must be because you've got a strong eye like Old Drumble."

"There you go again. Telling me I'm like a dog." His mother growled deep in her throat. "You watch out, John Jackman, or it'll be the last time you're allowed to set foot outside the back door, let alone go trotting down the road behind a mob of sheep." She barked and snapped her teeth at Jack, so he jumped backwards.

"But Old Drumble's got such a strong eye, he did see right through the swagger's hat, and he's got a first-class memory. He never forgets a face!"

"You don't have to go believing everything Andy tells you. He's a great one for picking up a bit here and a bit there, and stringing them together into a story. It's all on account of being on his own, wandering along behind the stock and talking to his horse and dogs to pass the time. I never believe half of what he tells me."

"How did Andy get to be a drover, Mum?"

"He didn't listen to his mother," said Mrs Jackman. "Like a certain little boy I know. And like all boys who don't listen to their mothers, he got into trouble.

"He started following mobs of sheep. First down to the bottom end of the street, then down to the next corner. Then he followed a mob to the next corner, and then over the railway crossing and down Cemetery Road. One day he just kept following a mob, forgot where home was, and never found his way back."

"Is that true?"

"He's still wandering around somewhere up in the middle of the North Island."

"True?"

"How would I know?" His mother stared at Jack with her strong eye, and he stared back. "Part of it might be true, and part might be made up." She watched Jack trying to understand that and put on her mysterious look.

"Andy started droving when he was a boy," she said, "about the turn of the century. There weren't the jobs then, the farm wasn't big enough for him and his brothers, and he was the youngest, so he went droving."

"How do you know?"

"His mother was some sort of second or third cousin to my mother, and I've known him all my life. Everyone knows Andy; he's been a character in the district since the year dot."

"What's the year dot, Mum?"

"Do you think I've got time to stand around talking to you all day? The housework isn't going to do itself. Ask your father, when he gets home from the factory for his lunch. He'll tell you some cock-and-bull story about what the year dot means."

Then, suddenly, his father was there, and the pie appeared from the oven in a gush of hot air, the edge of the pastry wavy, brown, and crisp, the little volcano puffing steam. Jack's mouth watered so much, he forgot to ask his father what the year dot meant.

"And don't you go getting flakes of pastry all over yourself," said his mother. "Oh, what's the use?"

Jack spent most of that afternoon climbing the lawsoniana hedge around the school horse paddock. Harry Jitters joined him, and they broke and bent the branches at the corner with Whites' Road till they'd made a hut.

Once the hut was finished, they tried sitting in it and saying how beaut it was, but they got a bit sick of doing that. So they tried to climb from one lawsoniana to the next without touching the ground, all the way from the corner to the gate into the school horse paddock at the other end. They'd have done it, too, but Harry gave a yell and fell off the top of a tree, grabbed hold of Jack, and they slid down the outside of the branches which dipped and dumped them on the ground.

"Down the road to the Domain," said Jack, "that paddock of Mr Lewis's that he closes up for hay, the lawsonianas are about a hundred feet high."

"Out on my Uncle Ken's farm, he's got lawsonianas two hundred feet high," said Harry.

"Do you think he'd let us slide down them?"

"He lets me do anything I like. One of his lawsonianas is about three hundred feet high, but that's a bit too high to slide down," Harry said.

"I slid down a lawsoniana five hundred feet high," Jack boasted. "Out Wardville. It took two hours to climb, and ten minutes to come down."

"That's not a true story, Jack Jackman. Everyone knows lawsonianas don't grow five hundred feet high!" said Harry Jitters. "It's not true . . . is it?"

"Part of it might be true, and part might be made up," said Jack, and tried to look mysterious.

"You just made it up!"

They crawled under the horse paddock gate, at the end where it was higher off the ground. "You'd think they'd fix the gate," said Jack, "so it doesn't leave so much of a gap."

"Why?"

"'Cause a horse could get down on his hands and knees and crawl under, like we just did."

"Aw! I'd like to see a horse that could crawl under a gate."

"I'll bet Nosy could!"

"Who's Nosy?"

"Nosy's Andy the Drover's horse. She can open gates, no trouble. The ones with a sliding latch, she just shoves along with her nose; the ones with a hook, she nudges them up with her nose, too. She's not so good with the hooks that have got a spring on them, but she's teaching herself, Andy reckons. He says it's just a matter of time before she finds out how to hold the spring open with one hoof and nudge the hook up with her nose."

"You're making up stories again."

"Andy said he left Nosy closed in for the night once, and she unhooked the gate, let herself out, went to the pub and got a skinful of beer, came home, let herself back into her paddock, and hooked the gate closed behind her. Andy wouldn't have known about it, but somebody told him he'd seen a horse drinking in the pub the night before, and they had trouble getting her out the door at closing time. She reckoned she hadn't finished her beer, but it was after six o'clock, so they threw her out.

"Andy had his suspicions, he reckoned, so he went to sniff her breath and smelled tobacco on her coat."

"Aw, everyone knows horses don't smoke!"

"I didn't say she'd been smoking, did I? Pubs are always full of smoke, so her coat stunk of it. But she'd been boozing all right, because Andy could still smell the beer on her breath next morning. What's more, Nosy was crook with the piss and no use for droving for a couple of days. Horses have terrible hangovers, because they're so big."

"Is that true?"

"Everything Andy says is true."

"Anyway, there's no pub in Matamata 'cause we're a dry area," Harry said, "and my mother says it's a good thing, too."

"I didn't say Matamata. It was over in Morrinsville.

63

They've got several pubs, as well as the saleyards, so Andy often has a droving job over there, and that's when Nosy opened the gate and got herself plastered, see!"

"Huh!" Harry grunted. "My mother says I'm not allowed to say 'plastered'. And you said 'piss', and that's swearing."

"Who are you going to tell?"

"I'm going to tell the vicar on you."

"I'm not scared of your silly old vicar. Anyway, next time Andy comes through, I'm going to help him drive his sheep all the way over the factory crossing and on to Cemetery Road."

"You are not!"

"Am so."

"Not."

"Am so."

"Am not."

"You said it! You said you're ham snot!"

"I am not ham snot!" said Harry Jitters and ran for home, while Jack Jackman did his puku dance in the middle of Ward Street and cried, "Unga-Yunga!"

Chapter Twelve

Why Jack Jumped Like a Sheep, How Old Nosy Put Waharoa on the Map, and Why Andy and Jack's Father Put Together a Stepladder Made out of Railway Sleepers.

ANDY BROUGHT SOME SHEEP through, the following morning, and Jack pestered his mother till she said he could go as far as the corner of Cemetery Road.

"You watch out for trains at the factory crossing," Mrs Jackman said. "Look both ways and, if you see one coming, you make sure you wait for it to go through before you cross." She had to call the last words after him, because Jack was already running out the gate.

"Can Old Drumble work cattle beasts just with his eye?" he asked Andy, as they crossed the Turangaomoana road to collect the mob. "Mum can work me through a closed door, just with her eye."

Andy nodded. "Old Drumble's eye's that strong, he can work anything."

"Anything?"

"Chooks. Goats. Pigs. I once saw him shift a loaded wagon five chains down the road, just using his strong eye. But that was for a bet, and he felt a bit dizzy afterwards, so I told him to lay off in case it made him crook."

"Could he work me?"

"You wouldn't like it if he did."

"Yes, I would. Please, Andy — make Old Drumble work me with his eye?" Jack grinned, excited.

They were standing by the hall. Andy made a little chirruping sort of whistle, nodded, and did something with his hand. Jack looked around to where he'd nodded, and saw Old Drumble staring at him.

Jack went to look away but found he didn't want to shift his eyes. He forgot Andy: he forgot the mob: he forgot Nosy. He stared back at Old Drumble who stared at him, lay down without taking his eyes off Jack's, kept his nose pointing straight at him, and crept forward about one inch. Then another.

Jack found himself stamping one foot at Old Drumble, the way he'd seen a ewe do it. Old Drumble hunched himself forward another inch. Jack backed away, but Old Drumble moved with him. Jack backed around Andy and Nosy, and Old Drumble came after him. For a second, Jack took his eyes off and ran, but there was a flash of black and white, and Old Drumble was there ahead of him, his eye fixed on Jack, daring him to move.

"I don't like this," Jack wanted to say, but the words wouldn't come out. Instead he backed around behind Nosy again, back past Andy, followed every step by Old Drumble holding him with his eye.

Jack took a quick glance, saw the gate up the side of the hall was open, and moved towards it. Old Drumble seemed to want him to go through it; Jack thought he could hear a voice telling him to go through it; he knew he wanted to go through it himself.

Jack jumped high through the gate, shouting "Baa!" like a sheep, and Old Drumble came over and lay down across the gateway, holding him inside. Andy whistled, and Old Drumble turned back into himself and let Jack out.

"I didn't like that," said Jack.

"Now you know what it feels like to be a sheep," said Andy, "being worked by an eye dog."

"It's a bit like the way Mum works me," Jack told him. "Has Old Drumble ever worked you?"

"Who do you think runs the show? I've been working for Old Drumble for years!

"I never wanted to be a drover, out on the road in all weathers. It was his idea." Andy shifted his hat so Jack saw his white skull for a moment, and then pulled it back down over his eyes.

"There's times I can't do a thing for myself because he turns his strong eye on me and makes me walk this way and that, round this corner, round that one. Take this road, not that one, I hear him saying, even though he hasn't spoken a word aloud.

"I told you Old Drumble's got a map of the North

Island inside his head. Just as well, too, because I never had much sense of direction myself."

Old Drumble led, the mob followed, and Young Nugget, Old Nell, Nosy, Andy, and Jack followed them. As they passed his house, Jack's mother came to the gate and said, "You watch out for trains, you hear me now?"

"I'll remind him," Andy nodded.

Then they were down the bottom end of Ward Street, Minnie Mitchell staring through her gate, and Harry Jitters hiding behind his mother's white azalea and not coming out till the mob was past. Jack didn't notice them; he was too busy watching Old Drumble's tail up the front of the mob, and listening to Andy.

"Did I ever tell you about the day I found Old Nosy up your mother's Granny Smith?" Andy asked.

"Nosy! How could she climb our apple tree?"

"Same way anyone climbs. No trouble to her. I was having a cup of tea with your mum and dad, and we heard this hullabaloo. It was Nosy up in the apple tree, that one in your backyard. She'd got up all right, but she found coming down a bit different."

"I got stuck up the apple tree once," said Jack. "Mum poked me with the broom handle, and that made me come down in a hurry. Then she gave me a spoonful of castor oil because I had the collywobbles from too many green apples."

"Well, you'll understand how Nosy felt. Cats are great

ones for getting stuck up trees. You know how they can climb anything? They'll get up high enough, and sit there, looking down and howling their heads off, till somebody's silly enough to bring a ladder, and climbs up and nearly breaks his neck trying to catch the cat, then it'll leap over him and run down the ladder, no trouble. And then it'll want a feed and hang around, rubbing against your legs and tripping you over. Cats!" Andy said. "It's a bit different when your horse gets stuck up a tree."

"What happened to Nosy?"

Andy whistled and raised his stick. Young Nugget cut back and stirred up a couple of sheep. "Like I was saying," said Andy, "she climbed up into your mother's apple tree and made a right pig of herself, stuffed herself full, then decided she wanted to come down, but didn't know how. Everyone in Waharoa came and had a look. A horse stuck up an apple tree!

"They sent photographers from the *Waikato Times* and the *Auckland Weekly News,* but the snaps didn't come out, or I'd show them to you. Still, there was something about her in the *New Zealand Herald* and the *Free Lance*. People said Nosy had put Waharoa on the map.

"She sat up there most of a week, and still didn't look like coming down."

"What'd she live on?"

"What do you think? Ate every single apple within reach by stretching out her long neck, and grabbing them between her teeth. Of course, she was too scared to let go of the branches, in case she fell."

Andy was quiet as they came to the church corner, and Old Drumble slowed the head of the mob, made sure the road was clear, and led them out and headed north.

Jack watched closely this time, and thought he saw how Old Drumble did it. He didn't say anything to the sheep, just pranced ahead with his tail in the air, and the sheep up the front followed it with their eyes and trotted after him. Not one of them ran the other way but, just in case, Old Nell scampered up the side of the mob and stood there, daring them to even think of it.

Jack and Andy followed along the main road. A lorry stopped, and Old Drumble turned, split the head of the mob, and the sheep trotted around either side.

"Thanks!" Andy nodded and winked back to the driver.

"You get some coots who want to drive through your mob," he said to Jack. "Haven't got time to wait. When that happens, Old Drumble pushes the mob together, and blocks the road deliberately. I've seen him keep an impatient driver waiting for a couple of hours, specially any clown who starts tooting and revving his engine. Old Drumble, he knows we've got the right of way on a stock route."

"What happened to Nosy, up in the apple tree?"

"Without her, I had no horse, so I put the mob I was

driving into the school footy paddock. Old Strap, the headmaster, wasn't too happy about it, but I'd driven stock for just about everyone on the school committee, and they reckoned it was okay.

"I camped in your back shed, and your father took a few days off from the factory and gave me a hand to put together a stepladder, out of railway sleepers. It had to be something pretty solid, because a horse weighs a fair bit, you know."

Jack nodded as if he already knew that a horse weighs a fair bit. "You'd need a big stepladder," he said. "Did Nosy come down it okay?"

Chapter Thirteen

How Nosy Came Down the Tree and
Got the Giant Farts, Guts for Garters,
Why Old Drumble Was a Fairly
Formal Sort of Dog, and Why Jack
Stuck His Feet Well Out to the Side.

"WE HAD THE STEPLADDER just about finished," said
Andy. "All it needed was handrails for Nosy to hang on
to, so she wouldn't slip over the side as she came down
out of the tree. Then, blow me days, if I didn't get up one
morning and found she'd jumped down out of the tree,
scoffed every dahlia in your mother's flowerbed, gobbled
your dad's cabbages, and chewed up every single one of
his onions. Three whole rows of them!

"Talk about pong! Her breath stunk like a thousand
years," said Andy. "Old Drumble let the mob out of the
school horse paddock, and we got on the road again, but
neither of us could stand it. Old Drumble made her walk
about half a mile behind the mob; he told her she had to
keep her mouth wide open, till the sun and the wind and
the rain washed away the stink of onions.

"I'll tell you what . . . "

"What?" asked Jack.

"Perhaps I'd better not say."

"Oh, tell me."

"No, you'll only get me into trouble, telling your mother."

"I won't!"

"Promise?"

"I promise," said Jack. "Cross my heart and hope to die," he said. He'd heard somebody say that, and it sounded pretty convincing.

Andy nodded. "Okay. Well, it's like this: because she'd eaten all those onions, Old Nosy got the giant farts!"

Jack laughed. "I didn't know horses fart!"

"Course they do," said Andy. "Worse than us. Specially when they've got the collywobbles from eating green apples for a week, and then they eat a stack of dahlias, cabbages, and three whole rows of onions. You ask your father. He saw it happen. But not a word about it to your mother."

The more Jack thought about Nosy having the giant farts, the more he laughed.

"It might sound funny now," said Andy, "but she stunk something terrible. People ran to close their windows, as I drove the mob past, and they shouted, 'Why don't you stand in the creek and give yourself a good scrub!' Somebody even yelled, 'Change your socks!' It was so embarrassing, I didn't know which way to look."

"Even though Nosy was half a mile behind the mob?" asked Jack.

"Even though she was half a mile back. She honked enough to knock a man off his feet. Once the wind swung round and carried her stench over us, and half the sheep dropped unconscious. It was just good luck that it changed direction again."

Jack nodded. "I'll try not to tell Mum," he told Andy, "but sometimes she can tell what I'm thinking."

"Don't even think about it," said Andy, "or your mother will have my guts for garters."

"I'll try not to," Jack promised, "but is it okay if I tell Dad?"

Andy nodded. "Jokers are more understanding," he said.

Jack climbed on the fence. Up there he could look over the heads of the mob at Old Drumble who'd stopped at the railway crossing and was looking first up the line and then down it in the other direction, making sure there was no train coming. As Jack watched, he stuck his tail up again and trotted ahead. The sheep followed him over the crossing and took the turn to the right down Cemetery Road. Old Nell moved up again, making sure none of them tried to head left around the factory road.

"Mum wouldn't know if I just went as far as Dunlops' gate with you," said Jack.

"I wouldn't try it on," Andy replied. "She's probably watching us with her strong eye, all the way down Ward

Street, straight through the church and the plantation, to where we're standing here."

"She can tell what I'm thinking through a closed door," said Jack.

"That's the sort of thing I mean. Uncanny, that's what it is!" Andy gave a whistle, and Old Drumble dived through the fence between the road and the railway line, trotted back, wriggled under the fence beside them, and looked up.

"Jack's about to head home," Andy told him. "How about shaking hands?"

Old Drumble sat and raised his front right paw. Jack gave it a shake. "Woof!" said Old Drumble.

"That's the way!" said Andy. "He's a fairly formal sort of a dog, Old Drumble. Hooray, Jack!"

"Hooray, Andy! Hooray, Old Drumble!"

Jack watched Old Drumble wriggle under the fence alongside the railway line, run along the track, jump through the fence again, and take the lead down Cemetery Road.

As Nosy passed Jack, she snorted at him and blew through her nostrils. "You should be ashamed of yourself," he told her. He sniffed but there wasn't any stink of onions, just the pleasant smell of horse and fresh-chewed grass. He stood a few minutes, watching her go, then thought of something and laughed out loud.

Mr Sunderland, pedalling home for lunch, thought

he was laughing at him and said something that Jack didn't hear. Jack looked both ways, crossed the railway lines and the main road, and trotted back towards the church corner. From there he could see Harry Jitters and Minnie Mitchell outside their gates, so started working his invisible dogs.

"That's a noisy huntaway you've got there," said his father's voice.

"Dad! I went with Andy and Old Drumble all the way to the corner of Cemetery Road, and Old Drumble shook hands, and he told me about the time Nosy climbed our apple tree and ate all the Granny Smiths and couldn't get down . . . " Jack ran out of breath.

"Did Old Drumble tell you all that?"

"Andy told me, but Old Drumble shook hands and said goodbye. And Andy told me how Nosy got down the tree after you'd built the stepladder out of railway sleepers, and she ate all your onions and got the giant farts."

Sitting on the bar of the bike, holding on to the handlebars, Jack felt his father shaking. "What's funny, Dad?"

His father laughed aloud. "I wouldn't go telling your mother about those giant farts. She mightn't think it was funny."

"Why doesn't she laugh at the same things we laugh at, Dad?"

"It's different for women, I suppose. They don't find farting funny, or they reckon they don't."

"But everybody farts, Dad. You told me so."

"All the same, your mother doesn't approve of it. So watch your tongue."

"Dad, how do you think Nosy climbed down out of the tree?"

"The same way you come down a telegraph post: held on to a branch with her teeth, felt with her back feet till she got a grip of the trunk, wrapped her legs around it, then let herself down backwards, a bit at a time."

"How do you know she came down like that?"

"At first, I couldn't work out how she'd managed it, so I climbed up and had a look, and there were her tooth marks round the branch. I got my own teeth round it, and felt for the trunk with my feet, hung on with my arms like Nosy must have done with her front legs, lowered my feet further down the trunk and took another grip, brought my arms down a bit, and shinned down like that."

"Did your teeth make marks around the branch, too?"

"Same as Nosy."

"I'm going to have a look when we get home."

"You won't find them. We both bit so hard, our teeth ringbarked that branch, and it died, so I sawed it off, next time I pruned the apple tree.

"Hello, Harry! Hello, Minnie!" Mr Jackman called.

"Hello, Mr Jackman!"

Jack didn't look at Harry and Minnie, but rang the bell to let them know he'd helped Andy drive the sheep all the way over the railway crossing to the corner of Cemetery Road, and shaken hands with Old Drumble, and he was getting a double home on his father's grid.

When Harry ran a few steps after them, Jack craned his head around for a look.

"Keep your feet out," said his father's voice. "You don't want to go sticking your toes into the spokes."

"What would that do, Dad?"

"There was a little boy up in Matamata getting a dub with his father, and he stuck his toes in the spokes and they were all chopped off."

"Crikey! Did it hurt?"

"You bet!"

"Did he die?"

"The quack stitched up where the toes had come off, and he got a job as a teller in the bank, where he can sit on a stool all day because feet without toes aren't much use for walking."

Jack watched the road ahead disappearing under the front wheel and stuck his feet well out because he didn't want to work in the bank.

"What did they do with the toes?"

"He went back on his crutches and had a look, but somebody said a dog had eaten them."

"Old Drumble wouldn't eat my toes."

"Keep your feet out of the way, and he won't have to."

Jack stuck his feet even further out.

Chapter Fourteen

How Jack Nearly Got His Mouth Washed Out With Soap, Why Mr Jackman Decided He'd Just Have to Take His Punishment, and Why Jack Couldn't Climb Down the Way that Nosy Did.

"DAD," JACK ASKED, "do you think Mum will let me go down Cemetery Road with Andy and Old Drumble, next time they come through?"

"So long as you don't tell her about Nosy having the giant farts, she might let you go. And I'd keep it to myself, about the way Nosy came down the apple tree."

"Why?"

"Your mother doesn't believe horses can climb apple trees."

"But she told me once that Nosy ate all her dahlias."

"Everyone knows horses love dahlias. But imagine what would happen if Mrs Dainty found out that some-one had seen a horse sitting up in Mum's Granny Smith, helping itself to the apples . . . "

"What?"

"You know Mrs Dainty. She'd go down to the post office, and the store, and the baker's, and the butcher's, and tell everybody how your mother had a horse up in her apple tree. Within a few hours, there wouldn't be another woman in Waharoa who'd give your mother the time of day."

"I'd show that Mrs Dainty!"

"That wouldn't help your mother."

"It's not fair!" Jack's voice rose high.

"It hasn't happened yet, and it's probably not going to."

"I know! What say we open Mrs Dainty's gate and let Nosy into her place? She could climb Mrs Dainty's Golden Delicious and eat all the apples. And everyone going down the Turangaomoana Road would see a horse up her apple tree, and then not a woman in Waharoa would give Mrs Dainty the time of day."

"It's an idea; but keep it up your sleeve in case we need it. And remember, not a word to your mother about Nosy and the giant farts, not unless you're looking for trouble."

Jack slipped off and opened the gate. His mother stood at the back door. "About time, too! I was just about to come out and look down the road for the pair of you. Another five minutes, and I'd have taken your lunch off the table!"

"Mum?" Jack said. "Next time, can I help Old Drumble and Andy take the mob down the end of Cemetery Road?"

"First it's just down the bottom of the street, then it's just as far as the church corner, and then just to the railway crossing. There's no satisfying the boy!"

Jack looked at his mother.

"We'll see," she said. "And what cock-and-bull story did Andy fill you up with this time?"

"He didn't tell me any cock-and-bull stories, Mum. He told me about how Nosy can climb trees, and how she comes down them." Jack looked at his father, who looked down at his plate and shook his head ever so slightly.

"She climbs telegraph posts, too." Jack looked desperate. "Once she climbed a lawsoniana five hundred feet high and slid down the outside."

"I've never heard such rubbish in all my life. Where does the man get such ideas?"

Jack picked at his lunch. Perhaps he'd better not say anything else. His father carved a crunchy bit off the cold meat, and put it on Jack's plate.

"Old Drumble," said Jack. "He climbs trees, too, only he gets stuck up in the branches and doesn't know how to come down. He sits up there and barks, and Andy has to ride Nosy underneath, stand on her back, and lift Old Drumble down."

"Eat your lunch," said Jack's mother. "I don't suppose you noticed if Mrs Mitchell's rose is out, the one on her front fence?"

"I meant to tell you," Mr Jackman said quickly. "It's got a couple of buds opening."

"Old Drumble eats roses," Jack told his mother. "Can I go down as far as the railway crossing by the cemetery, next time Andy comes through?"

"And how do you think you're going to get home, from right down at the cemetery crossing? If I know you, you'll find a horse sitting up a tree, stop to help it climb down, and forget your way home."

"I'll have a word with Andy," said Mr Jackman. "If he's going to be at the cemetery crossing about midday, I can get away a couple of minutes early, bike down there, give Jack a double, and we'll still be home in time for lunch. Now, I'd better get back to work before the one o'clock whistle blows."

Jack watched his father put the bicycle clips on his trouser cuffs, so they wouldn't get caught in the chain. "Be careful you don't say anything else," said Mr Jackman. "You know, about . . . Goodbye, dear!" he called and rode off.

Halfway down Ward Street, he caught up to Mr Sunderland.

"I saw young Jack at the crossing, midday," said Mr Sunderland.

"He'd been giving Andy the Drover a hand," Mr Jackman told him.

"He laughed at me. I've no idea why."

"Andy told him a story about that mare of his, Nosy, about her climbing up an apple tree, and being unable to get down, and Jack would have been laughing to himself about her."

Mr Sunderland grinned. "That Andy tells some yarns!" They rode on together.

Back home, Jack was giving his mother a hand, drying the dishes. "And she ate all your dahlias, Andy said. And all your roses, and Dad's cabbages."

"I don't know about the roses. But somebody left the gate open once, and she got in and ate my dahlias, and your father's cabbages."

Jack laughed, polished a plate with the tea towel, and said, "And she ate all Dad's onions and farted. Giant farts."

"Are my ears deceiving me? Did I hear you say—? No, there's no need to go repeating it. If I hear you using language like that again, I'll wash out your mouth with soap, young man.

"Are you trying to rub the pattern off that plate? Put it in the cupboard and get another. At the rate you're going, the dishes will dry themselves."

"Mum, why don't we just let them dry themselves? It'd be a lot easier."

"First you start off with horses climbing trees, then you use bad language, and next thing you're wanting the dishes to dry themselves. No, you've said quite enough for one day. And don't let me hear you even think of using that word again."

When the five o'clock whistle went, Jack trotted down Ward Street to meet his father. "Mum's going to wash out your mouth with soap," he told him, "for teaching me to say 'fart'. She went off pop and reckons she's going to show you."

"You didn't go telling your mother I taught you to say 'fart'?" Jack's father jammed on his brakes, skidded, and turned the bike into Whites' Road. "We'd better go down the bush and hide in Mr Weeks's sawdust heap where the old mill used to stand. Mum won't think of looking for us there." He pedalled a couple of chains. "I thought I told you not to say 'fart' in front of her?"

"It just sort of popped out by itself. Dad, won't Mum be lonely without us?"

"I suppose she will. Perhaps we'd better go home, and I'll just have to take my punishment." Mr Jackman turned and pedalled back to the corner of Ward Street.

"What'll she do?"

"I suppose she'll thrash me."

"She wouldn't thrash you, Dad."

"Well, you'd better not say fart again, or she might."

His father felt Jack's grip loosen on the handlebars. "Were you scared?" he asked.

"Just a bit." Jack thought and said, "Mr Weeks keeps his bull in the paddock next to the sawdust heap."

"Who are you more scared of: your mother, or Mr Weeks's bull?"

"Mum!" said Jack.

"Me, too," said his father, and Jack rang the bell. He was pleased they weren't going to hide in the sawdust heap after all, but he didn't say so.

He waited a while to see what his mother did to his father, but she said nothing, so he went out and climbed the apple tree. Several branches had been sawn off, but he thought he could tell which one Nosy had bitten. He tried biting a branch himself, but nearly fell out of the tree. When he had a go at lowering himself, the trunk was too thick for him to get his legs around. Besides, there were too many branches in his way.

The apple tree didn't have a straight trunk like a telegraph pole, so it must have grown a fair bit since the day Nosy climbed it and couldn't get down again. When he heard his name called, he swung down and ran inside.

"What's for tea, Mum?"

"I've minced the last of the cold meat and made a hash. Just look at those hands! You see you give them a good scrub. There's no call for you to come to the table looking like a savage. And tell your father his tea's ready; he's got his nose buried in that paper of his. Come on, the pair of you. I'm not going to tell you again."

Chapter Fifteen

Why Old Drumble Could Dive
Through Fences, How Jack Got His
Nose Pulled, and Why Mr Jackman Said
He'd Bark at Minnie Mitchell.

IT WAS STILL LIGHT after they finished doing the dishes, so Jack wandered down Ward Street to where Harry Jitters was throwing stones at the telegraph post on the corner. They hit it twice, both of them, then had a look at their hut in the hedge, but it was dark under the lawsonianas. When Jack groaned, Harry shrieked and skinned his knee diving through the fence, instead of climbing over the strainer post.

"Old Drumble dives through fences, no trouble," said Jack. "He can see how far apart the wires are, because he's an eye dog."

"Is that what an eye dog means?"

"That, and having a strong eye so he can head sheep. My mother's got a strong eye, too. She can dive through fences. And she can tell what I'm thinking through a closed door."

"Mine, too," said Harry.

"My mother can head sheep with her strong eye," said Jack.

"Mine, too."

"Mine can see what I'm thinking all the way down Ward Street, straight through the church and the plantation, and as far as the corner of Cemetery Road."

"Aw!"

"True! Andy the Drover told me. She can tell what we're saying to each other right now. It's her strong eye."

"You reckon she can hear us now?"

"No trouble. Eye dogs can hear things that people can't. They've got strong ears as well as strong eyes. My mother's got strong ears."

"Mine, too," said Harry. "I bet my mother's listening to what we're saying now."

It was getting dark. From down the end of the street, the bottom end, came the sound of Mrs Jitters's voice calling, "Harry!" Jack looked startled. "Harry!" came the voice again. "Time you came in, Harry!"

Without a word to Jack, Harry Jitters turned and trotted down to his end of the street. Jack looked after him, feeling lonely. "Coming!" Harry called to his mother, invisible in the gloom.

Jack turned and headed home. Halfway to the top end of Ward Street, he heard his own name through the dusk. "Time you came inside!" his mother called, and Jack nodded and smiled to himself as he trotted towards the sound.

"I'll show you how an eye dog works," he told Harry Jitters, next morning. "But, first you've got to kneel on the ground. Okay. Now, think you're a sheep and go 'Baa!'"

"Why?"

"Do you want to see how an eye dog works or not?"

"Oh, all right." Harry screwed up his face, thought he was a sheep, and went, "Baa!"

Jack dropped to the ground, crouched with his body in a straight line, his nose pointing at Harry's, and stared with his strong eye.

Harry tried laughing, but Jack took no notice. He kept staring at him, and moved one hand forward an inch, then the other.

"What's the matter?" asked Harry. "You trying to look like a dog or something?" But Jack held his eye with his own and didn't move. Harry tried to wriggle to one side, but Jack was there, staring at him, harder than ever. Harry backed away.

"Oh, come on, Jack," he said. But Jack inched forward, eyes fixed on Harry's.

"What're you supposed to be looking at?" Harry put his hand to his throat. He could feel Jack's eyes. "I'm not playing this stupid game," said Harry, getting to his feet, but Jack was already standing, still staring into his eyes and creeping forward. Harry reached behind and felt for the gate. Jack lifted his lip and Harry saw the tips of his teeth. It was too much.

Harry backed into the fence and felt the jab of rose thorns. He turned away, swung back, felt Jack's gaze, and leapt for the gate, feeling for it with his hand, but it wasn't there. He heard a noise, a bit like the baa of a sheep, and wondered where it was coming from. Then his hand found the gap. He leapt through it, and Jack slammed the gate shut behind him.

"Anyway, I wasn't scared of you, Jack Jackman," Harry went to say, but Jack ran out his tongue between his front teeth, like a dog panting. Harry was saved by the sound of the kitchen window opening behind him.

"You boys go down the street if you want to make a lot of noise. Don't go knocking my rose around, Harry. I saw you run into it." A hand stuck out the window, waving a sugarbag oven cloth. "Off you go at once, the pair of you!"

Jack had vanished into the hedge at the sound of Mrs Jitters's voice, and Harry had to look for him. "Who taught you to be an eye dog?" he asked, but Jack didn't describe how Old Drumble had backed him through his own gate.

"Old Drumble taught me," he said. "Only a strong-eyed dog can teach you, and it takes years to learn."

Just then, Minnie Mitchell came out her gate to see what all the noise was about. Harry saw her and had an idea. "Try it on her," he said. "Show her how an eye dog works."

"I heard you," said Minnie. "What are you two whispering about? Anyway, what's an eye dog?"

She was about five or six paces outside her gate when Jack fixed her with his strong eye. He lifted one front foot and stood frozen, pointing straight at Minnie, the way Old Drumble stood pointing straight at a sheep. Just for a moment, Jack wished he had a tail like Old Drumble's, so he could lay it out straight in line with the rest of his body. He stared at Minnie's eyes and went to take another step forward.

"Who do you think you're staring at, Jack Jackman?" Minnie stamped like one of the ewes that Jack had seen try to stand up to Old Drumble's stare. Next moment, Jack knew, she'd baa, whirl, and run like an old ewe. He frowned, put all his power into his eye, took another step straight towards her, and Minnie Mitchell leapt forward and pulled his nose.

"Don't you look at me like that, Jack Jackman. What do you think you're doing?"

It took a lot of explaining, and Jack felt very uncomfortable under Minnie's accusing stare, but Harry managed to convince her that Jack was just trying to be an eye dog, working sheep with his strong eye. Minnie got the idea quickly; she worked Harry back through his gate and shut it behind him; then she turned her strong eye on to Jack and said he'd better get home unless he wanted his nose pulled again.

As he trotted home, Jack looked back and saw Minnie staring after him. He would have tried barking at her, but she got the idea first and barked at him, and Jack turned and scampered up the top end of Ward Street. Somehow, things hadn't gone quite right.

"You've got a face as long as my arm," said his mother. "What's the matter now?"

"Me'n Harry Jitters were playing eye dogs."

"Harry Jitters and I!"

"I was playing eye dogs with Harry Jitters, and I backed him through his gate, and Minnie Mitchell come out and pulled my nose."

"Came out. What did you do to make a nice girl like Minnie do that?"

"Nothing. I was just eyeing her, to make her go back inside her gate."

"Well, I don't blame Minnie. No girl wants to be stared at as if she's a sheep and backed through her gate."

"Yes, but suddenly she turned into an eye dog and backed Harry through his gate, and then she turned into a huntaway and pulled my nose and told me it was time I was getting home unless I wanted my nose pulled again. And when I looked back, she barked at me. Girls don't know how to play."

His mother grinned. "And you put your tail between your legs and ran home?"

Jack looked down and shuffled.

"You'd better start learning that's no way to treat a girl. The idea! Staring at her, and backing her through her gate."

"But I didn't. She eyed me, same as you do. Then she turned into a huntaway and barked at me. You can't be a heading dog and a huntaway all at once. Everybody knows that."

"Well, next time you'd better bark first. Now, wash your hands. Before I know where I am, your father will be home expecting his lunch to be on the table."

They were eating lunch, when Jack's father said, "Your friend Minnie Mitchell barked at me, just now, as I rode past her place."

"She thinks she's smart, but she doesn't know the difference between a heading dog and a huntaway. Girls never play fair."

"As I ride back to work," said his dad, "I'll bark at her, before she can bark at me."

"That's what I'll do, too," said Jack. "Would you bark at her real loud, Dad?"

Chapter Sixteen

Why Jack's Father Barked, What His Mother Thought About Having Strong Ears, and Ten Bob on the Two-Year-Old's Nose.

"ARE MY EARS DECEIVING ME? Barking at girls! You'll do nothing of the sort, my lad," said his mother. "And what sort of example do you think you're setting the boy? You'll be giving the top end of Ward Street a bad name, the pair of you.

"Jack, if you've finished playing around with your lunch, you can go out and pick up all the leaves under the cabbage tree. I don't want to see a single one on the lawn.

"And, as for you, talking of barking at a little girl, isn't it time you got back to your work before the whistle blows?"

Mr Jackman grinned at Jack, said goodbye to his wife, and got on his bike. As he went out the gate, he winked at Jack under the cabbage tree, barked once, and Jack barked back.

The kitchen window popped open. His mother's head stuck out. "Did I hear you barking?"

"It was Dad."

"I'll show that man! What are you staring at? Get on with those leaves. And when you've picked them all up, you can put them on the compost heap. And if I hear so much as another yap, I'll buckle dog collars round both your necks, chain the pair of you to the clothes-line, and you can have a bone for your tea tonight."

That afternoon, Mrs Jackman went down to the bottom end of Ward Street to have a look at the Crimson Glory rambler that Mrs Jitters had flowering. "She's going to give me a cutting, this winter," she said to Jack when she came home. "How dare you tell Harry Jitters your mother has strong ears? I thought I told you: I'm not some sort of dog!"

"I just told Harry you can see through doors and hear what I'm thinking. I was trying to train him as a huntaway."

"Yes, well, I don't think Mrs Jitters wants her son growing up to be a noisy sort of dog. I don't know what the world's coming to — dogs barking and eyeing each other up and down Ward Street. Talking of dogs, look who's tying up his horse— "

Jack didn't need to be told who it was. He tore out. Nosy was already trying to undo her reins off the fence, and Old Drumble was holding a mob of sheep the other side of the hall corner.

"I'm training a heading dog and a huntaway down the

bottom end of the street," Jack told Andy, who nodded as he took a sugarbag filled with bits and pieces from the pikau behind his saddle.

"It's a good idea to have a young dog coming on," Andy said. "You never know when you're going to need him. Just this morning, that Young Nugget nearly got himself skittled as we came round the back of Matamata. Some coot in a cut-down Model A, careering along Burwood Road, doing the better part of thirty miles an hour, not looking where he's going and, the next thing, he near ploughs into my mob. Young Nugget leaps out of the way, just in time.

"Old Drumble keeps the mob bunched while I give the driver a piece of my mind. I tells him, 'It would have cost you a tenner to run over Young Nugget, twenty-five quid for Old Nell, and you hit Old Drumble — the sky's the limit!'

"Here we are," he said to Jack's mother, "a cutting out of Mrs Kevin Ryan's garden, some plum chutney from Mrs Bryce, and the recipe for Mrs Oulds's seed cake, the one she said you admired at the church Bring and Buy. And these here are from old Tom McGuire out Okoroire, seed potatoes — Maori Chief. Old Tom says they're a good cropper, and they stand up against the blight better than most.

"'As good a tatie as Oi've tasted since Oi came out here from Oireland, just a spalpeen no taller than halfway

95

up the hoight of a donkey's shin,' he told me. Of course, he swears Irish spuds tasted better than ours because they used to dig in seaweed. Enough kelp, and you never had to add salt to the spuds, so he reckons. Now, I wonder if that's true, or did he just kiss the Blarney Stone? What do you suppose, Jack?"

But Jack was too busy watching Andy's scalp appear as his hat came off. Also, he was waiting to ask his mother the question that she knew he had trembling on the tip of his tongue.

And, because she knew he wanted to ask it, she didn't look at him, but busied herself filling the teapot from the kettle on the stove, getting the milk from the safe, the sugar bowl, a teaspoon, and setting out some ginger-nuts on a plate. And all the time exclaiming over the cuttings, the recipe, the seed potatoes, swapping gossip and news, asking questions of Andy, and telling him what she'd got for him to drop in to others along his road.

"No, it's too late," she said, when Jack went to open his mouth. "You're certainly not going down to the cemetery crossing with Andy. It's far too far for somebody who's silly enough to let a little girl pull his nose. Besides, your father's gone back to work, and there's no way he could bike down and give you a double home."

"Aw!" Jack's voice rose to a whine.

"That's quite enough of that, my boy. There'll be plenty more opportunities to go down to the cemetery crossing. I'm not promising anything, mind you. We'll see when the time comes."

"Can I go as far as the factory crossing today, like last time?"

"I suppose so, but only if Andy can be bothered taking you."

Jack followed Andy out, grinning at Old Drumble's tail waving ahead of the mob, saying hello to Old Nell and Young Nugget, rubbing Nosy's nose when she put it down to him.

"Just as far as the corner of Cemetery Road," his mother called from the front porch, "and not a step further. You hear me now?"

Jack waved, and Andy touched his hat. They walked in silence, Jack's feet feeling the Smarter Pills that covered the road and sniffing the ammoniac air.

"Did I ever tell you," said Andy, "about the time Old Drumble made me take him to the Te Aroha Races?"

"No."

"We're riding out to pick up a mob one day and, going past the racecourse, Old Drumble stops dead in his tracks in the middle of the road and, before I can open my mouth, he's turned his strong eye on me. Next thing I know, he's backing me and Old Nosy through the gate and into the racecourse. I didn't have any say in it.

"We wanders over to have a look at the racehorses dancing around and getting themselves worked up in the birdcage, and Old Drumble catches me eye and nods at a two-year-old gelding who's starting for the first time. Next thing I know, I'm being backed across to put on a bet. I know what he means by that nod, so I puts ten bob on the two-year-old's nose."

Andy whistled, but already Old Nell was streaking along to guard an open gate. Past her, Jack saw Harry and Minnie dive inside and slam their gates behind them.

"Why did you put ten bob on the gelding's nose?"

"You think a horse is going to come in first, so you put your bet on his nose — for a win. If you put it on for a place — coming second or third — you get paid less. Five bob each way means you're putting five bob on for a win, and five bob for a place. It still costs ten bob, but you're not sure it'll win, so you're sort of covering yourself."

"Did the gelding win?"

"The clodhopping goorie!" Andy's voice creaked, dry with dust. "The leaders are turning into the back straight, and he's half a furlong behind the rest of the field. I looks down in disgust at Old Drumble, but he's vanished. He told me to bet on the mongrel; now he's too embarrassed to hang around and look a man straight in the eye.

"There used to be some weeping willows, the other side of the Te Aroha course, that hid a couple of chains of the back straight. By the time the leaders come out from behind the willows, the gelding's in front! How in the name of all that's wonderful did he catch up so fast? The crowd roars. He comes thundering down past the stand, past the judges, wins by a nose."

"That's the nose with the bet on it?" asked Jack.

Andy nodded. "He didn't just win, but he caught up from away behind the field — in record time. Just about everyone's done their money, but nobody's worried; they're all too busy screaming and yelling that New Zealand's found a new Phar Lap."

Chapter Seventeen

Why Minnie Mitchell Looked Like a Dying Goldfish, Why Jack Sat on His Tail as He Galloped Home, and Why He Stood on One Leg and Havered.

"Everyone's over the moon because of the unknown gelding winning the race," said Andy the Drover.

"Up on the members' stand, the cockies' wives are dancing in their best silk dresses, jumping out of their high-heeled shoes, and waving their silly hats. And the cockies in their brown pinstripe suits, with their members' tickets jiggling from their waistcoat buttonholes, they're jigging and tossing betting slips, hats, and race cards in the air. Old Tom Mihi from Manawaru throws up his field glasses, and they come down and knock him out cold.

"They're all so busy cheering the gelding, I'm probably the only person watching the jockey. The other horses slow down, and the steward rides out to lead the winner in, but the gelding's going too fast to pull up. Round the first bend he goes on a victory lap. Along the back straight, he disappears behind the weeping willows, and there's a pause."

Andy's voice dropped, so Jack looked up. "The gelding

must have slowed down behind the trees, then he comes trotting round the bend into the home straight, dancing sideways past the members' stand, showing off, snorting and tossing his head. The crowd goes even wilder. The steward takes the reins from the jockey, so he can wave back to the crowd, and leads him in to unsaddle.

"And just at that moment, Old Drumble appears beside me again, grinning away to himself and panting real heavy. He says nothing — a man can see he's got no breath — just runs out his tongue and licks his chops.

"The announcement comes," said Andy. "Five hundred quid for a win! I must be the only one who put anything on the gelding, apart from his owner. And I've got ten bob on his nose; I should have bet a fiver.

"I lines up at the payout window, all by meself, and the crowd claps and cheers. I collects me two hundred and fifty nicker, stuffs it down me shirt, gets on Nosy, and I'm away down the road to pick up me sheep, Old Drumble trotting alongside and looking as if butter wouldn't melt in his mouth."

"If he's that good at picking winners, why didn't you stay and have another bet?"

"Old Drumble's no good at picking winners."

"But he picked the gelding . . . "

"It wouldn't have won on its own. It was coming last, remember, as they went into the back straight. Jack, me boy, I was the only person on the course that day who realised the skulduggery that was going on. Everyone else was so busy cheering and waving as the gelding went past the post: I was the only one there who looked at the jockey."

"The jockey?"

"That wasn't no jockey. When he stood up in his stirrups and flogged the gelding past the post, I sees something he's been sitting on, to keep it hidden. A bushy tail!

"Like I said, nobody else sees it because they're all too busy watching the amazing horse. But I watches the jockey go past, crouched high, his eyes bulging out so far they look like motor-bike goggles, and he's leaning forward and barking in the gelding's ear what he's going to do to him if he doesn't win. That was when I saw his bushy tail.

"You mean . . . "

"I mean that jockey was Old Drumble! He'd nicked across the course, waited in the weeping willows, pulled off the jockey, used his strong eye on the gelding, barked in his ear, and scared him into winning. That's why he galloped him round on a victory lap, jumped off behind the willows, so the jockey could get on again and ride him in to unsaddle."

"Can Old Drumble ride a horse?"

"Never seen a rider to match him."

"What about the real jockey?"

"He wasn't going to tell anyone the truth, was he?

Everyone was slapping him on the back for riding the new Phar Lap.

"Lucky the stewards didn't notice it was Old Drumble riding. They'd have banned him off the course for life, me and Nosy along with him.

"Now, I've never told that story to another soul, Jack, and Old Drumble wouldn't want it to get around that he rode the winner, so you'd best keep it to yourself. Even though it happened years ago, people who went to the Te Aroha races that day might kick up a row and want their money back."

Jack nodded.

"There's something else. Ever since he eyed that gelding into running first," said Andy, "I've kept Old Drumble away from racecourses. If they found out he'd ridden a winner, every owner in the country with a promising young nag would want him to ride for them. And how about my sheep and cattle that need— What on earth's wrong with that girl?"

"That's Minnie Mitchell," Jack said.

"Yes, but why's she hiding behind her gate, opening and shutting her mouth like a dying goldfish?"

"She thinks she's a heading dog," Jack explained, "but she's really a huntaway. Mind you," he said, glancing at Minnie Mitchell and looking away quickly, "she's got a pretty strong eye."

"Okay, but what's wrong with her mouth?"

"She's barking," said Jack, "silently, so she doesn't upset the sheep."

"What about him?" Andy asked, nodding at Harry Jitters.

"He's a bit mixed up, too," said Jack. "He's a huntaway who can't bark, and he wants to be a heading dog, but he's got no eye."

"Well, that's the way the cards fall," said Andy, giving Minnie and Harry a nod. "We'd all like to be different from what we are. Look at Old Drumble. He could have been a top jockey, but he's better off as a leading dog. How about nicking up the front of the mob, and giving him a hand to turn them out on to the main road when we come to the church corner?"

Jack's face shone.

"Just walk half a step behind him, and do what he does. He'll let you know if you put a foot wrong."

Nothing was coming either way, so Old Drumble led the mob out on to the main road at the church corner, and Jack walked half a step behind. Jack was dying to ask Old Drumble about the time he rode a winner at Te Aroha, but held his tongue. Over the factory crossing they went, and Old Nell came up and cut off the road around the back of the factory, as Old Drumble turned right into Cemetery Road.

Jack stopped at the corner. He could feel his right foot itching, but the thought of his mother saying "Not a step further!" stopped it in mid-air. The last of the mob trotted past, then came Young Nugget, and then Andy and Nosy.

"See you next week," Andy called. "Tuesday morning. We'll be there in good time for your father to pick you up, down at the cemetery crossing." Nosy shook her head till the bit jangled, flapped her ears at Jack, and they were gone.

Jack watched them go, looked both ways up and down the railway lines, then crossed and trotted home with his tail in the air, leading a huge mob of sheep. At the bend in Ward Street, he turned into a huntaway just in time to bark vociferously at Harry and Minnie as they came out of their gates. His change was so sudden, his bark so loud, they dived back inside, and Jack turned into a jockey and galloped the rest of the way up Ward Street, sitting on his tail — to hide it — and overtaking the field at Te Aroha.

Halfway home, he leaned forward and barked into his horse's ear. A young gelding, it got such a scare, it leapt ahead to thunder past the winning post.

Tuesday morning, and Andy came at last. Jack ran outside, said hello to Nosy and looked at Old Drumble holding a mob on the grass. He ran inside, but his mother and Andy were talking on and on about this one and that, whether Mrs Arnold's youngest was over the croup, whether the whooping cough out Soldiers' Settlement

Road was going to spread through the district, who was the new postmaster at Walton, and did he have a family?

Jack stood on his right leg and rubbed the back of it with his left foot. He tried standing on his left leg and rubbing the back of it with his right foot. He ran outside and ran inside again.

"Stop havering," his mother told him.

"But, Mum . . ."

At last, Andy finished his cup of tea, put on his hat, and picked up his sugarbag, now loaded with an ivory crochet hook for old Mrs Gray; a knitting pattern for a Fair Isle jersey for young Mrs Feak, one that she'd find would use up all those leftover bits of different-coloured wool; and a recipe for Christmas cake made with dry ginger ale instead of brandy for Mrs Killeen, whose husband belonged to the Plymouth Brethren and wouldn't have so much as an eggcupful of strong drink in the house.

Jack swallowed.

Chapter Eighteen

Looking As Silly as a Chook Running Around With Its Head Chopped Off, How to Get an Idea of Where the Pipiroa Ferry Is, and Why Sheep Don't Like Rivers.

As WELL AS THE SUGARBAG filled with things for other people, Andy had several bits of news and gossip to deliver along the road, a cellophane-covered jar of tart marmalade made with poorman's oranges for himself, and a Bushells tea tin filled with ginger-nuts.

Jack looked at his mother. "Can I go with Andy?"

His mother looked back. "Go where?"

"As far as the cemetery crossing."

"As far as the cemetery crossing?"

"You promised."

"I did nothing of the sort. I just said that we'd see when the time came."

Jack stood on his right leg, eyed his mother, and held his breath. "And tell old Mrs Gray for me, I'll pop in when I can, early next week," his mother said to Andy. "Why are you staring like that?" she asked Jack. "Looking as silly as a chook running around with its head chopped off."

"She's enjoying your fruit cake," Andy nodded. "Likes to have a piece with a cup of tea, she reckons."

Jack wriggled and stood on his left leg.

"Mum!" he said in a strangled voice, as Andy headed for the back door.

"He can come with you just as far as the cemetery crossing and not another step further," his mother said to Andy. And she said to Jack, "If your father's not there, you're to turn and run back to the factory corner, but you'll probably meet him before you get that far.

"Just as far as the cemetery crossing, you hear me? You can watch them on to the main road, but don't you dare put a foot on the lines. We don't want you run over by a goods train hurtling through, the way they do. There, the boy's gone without even listening to a word I said . . . "

Jack skipped a couple of steps, saw Young Nugget look at him, walked soberly, glanced at Andy, and wondered if he'd ever have dry leathery lines and folds on his own face.

"Maybe," he thought to himself, "maybe if I rub a handful of dust into my cheeks, I might look like that, too. Maybe if I ate some dust, I'd sound dry and creaky, too."

As if he knew what Jack was thinking, Andy creaked and asked him, "Did I ever tell you about the time me and Old Drumble were driving a mob of sheep across the Hauraki Plains, and we struck trouble at the Pipiroa ferry?"

Jack looked over the heads of the mob at Old Drumble's tail and shook his head. "Where's Pipiroa?"

"You know how, if you go down behind the factory, you come to the Waharoa Creek?"

"Dad's going to take me eeling down the creek."

"Think of a globe of the world," said Andy. "Now, follow the creek down far enough, you'll come to the bridge on the Walton road; go on down past Ngarua, and she becomes the Waitoa River; and down past Springdale, the Waitoa becomes the Piako; and the Piako runs down past Patetonga, Ngatea, Pipiroa, and into the Firth of Thames; and north the Firth opens into the Hauraki Gulf; and, north again and you're into the Pacific Ocean. All by following down the Waharoa Creek.

"North you go, Jack, over the equator, north again up the North Pacific and over the top of the North Pole and head downhill, and you're into the North Atlantic Ocean; and you keep coming south over the equator, down the South Atlantic, down to the South Pole, across the Antarctic; and there you are at the bottom of the South Pacific; and you head north and uphill, up the east coast of New Zealand, and turn left into the Hauraki Gulf, and up the Firth of Thames, and up the Piako River, past Pipiroa, upstream and under the bridge on the Walton road, up the creek till you're down behind the factory, and you're back in Waharoa and Ward Street.

"You've gone up and over the North Pole and back up

to Waharoa over the South Pole. That should give you an idea of where the Pipiroa ferry is, just upstream of the Piako mouth."

"Some day," said Jack, "I'm going to go right around the world that way."

Andy crooked a finger at a couple of sheep falling off to one side, and Young Nugget chivvied them back into the flock.

"Heading down the main road from Auckland to the Thames," Andy said, "you cross the Piako on the Pipiroa ferry, then you come to the Waihou River with Orongo this side and Kopu on the other."

Jack listened to the names and wrote what they sounded like on the map he was drawing inside his head.

"At the time I'm talking of," said Andy, "they haven't built the long bridge at Kopu yet, so there's a barge for taking stock across the Waihou. But at Pipiroa, there's just the ferry, and stock have to take their turn with the lorries, and carts, and the occasional car.

"I've promised to pick up some sheep near Kaiaua, up the Miranda coast, drive them across the Plains, and up the Thames coast, to where they're breaking in a block up the Tapu Valley. The cocky's clearfelled, burnt off, and sown in bush-burn seed. He's had a good take of grass, but the fern comes up, too, so he puts on steers to crush it, and to compact the soil.

"Now the steers have done their job, he wants to unload them and put on sheep, and that's where me and Old Drumble come in. We'll deliver his sheep, then turn around and drive his steers up to the Auckland sales. But the cocky can't take the steers off till he gets the sheep, or the fern's going to get away on him. So he's been on my hammer to get cracking.

"Crossing the Plains, we get the sheep as far as Pipiroa. It's been howling from the nor-east, and a scow's got herself blown into the mouth of the Piako and stranded fair in the middle of the channel, so the ferry can't get across."

Jack nodded. Harry Jitters and Minnie Mitchell were watching from behind their gates as he drove the mob past. Up at the head, Old Drumble's tail stopped, and the sheep in front stopped, too, as a lorry carrying posts and battens rattled along the main road through Waharoa.

Andy nodded at the lorry. "Going out Wardville, to Percy West's," he said. "Jerry Patch's bull flattened half the boundary fence between their places, strainers and all. Tore them out of the ground, smashed and tossed them around like kindling wood. That old Jerry Patch, he's too mean to do anything about fixing the fence; besides, he's scared of his own bull, so Percy reckons he'd better do the job himself.

"'I'll take the cost of it out of Jerry's hide,' he told

me. 'Run my herd on his paddocks, while I'm doing the fencing. It's going to cost him twice as much in grazing as it would have done if he'd coughed up his share for a few chains of fence.'"

"What about Old Drumble and the Pipiroa ferry?" Jack asked.

"Taihoa," said Andy. "I'm coming to that.

"Well, you know, sheep aren't all that keen on swimming. You can put them across a river, but you want a shallow beach to get them into the water, a shallow place the other side, to get them out, and you've got to have a current that carries them in the right direction. Besides, these ones we're driving across the Plains, they're carrying a bit of wool.

"When we reach Pipiroa, the tide's high and just starting to turn. In a few minutes, she'll be ripping out. Put the sheep in there, they'll finish up on Waiheke Island.

"Old Drumble leaves the mob bunched up, and goes to have a talk with the ferry skipper. 'We'll never get them across on the ferry,' he comes back and tells me. 'Not till they shift that scow, and she's got a deck-load of sand that they'll have to barrow over the side to lighten her.'

"The dirty-brown water moves and swirls down the channel, carrying a mangrove berry, twigs, leaves, grass, and a drowned ewe from upstream. Luckily, Old Drumble spots it and turns the mob around facing the way we've come, till the carcass vanishes downstream. He's got a pretty wise head on him for a dog."

Andy grinned down at Jack and said, "While he's got the mob looking the other way, I says to him, 'We can't muck around here, waiting for them to get the scow out of the way.'

"Old Drumble nods. 'I've got an idea,' he tells me. He turns the mob again, and moves it forward till they're standing above the river, baa-ing and stamping, a bit nervous. They hadn't seen the carcass drift by, but they don't like rivers, sheep, and you can't blame them, specially if they're carrying a bit of wool."

"I wouldn't blame them," said Jack.

Chapter Nineteen

Why the Seagulls Fell Dead Out of the Air,
Why Andy Gave the Swagger the Marmalade
and Ginger-Nuts, and Why Townies Don't
Know How to Look After Themselves.

"A COUPLE OF THEM cunning blighters of sheep," said
Andy to Jack, "they're standing on the bank of the Piako,
looking as if they're about to turn and stampede away
from the river. I'm keeping me eye on one leery old ewe,
when there's an almighty, thundering bark shakes the
ground under me feet.

"You might find this hard to believe, Jack, but that
thundering bark's so loud, a couple of seagulls fold their
wings and drop komaty out of the air, and the Piako River
gets such a fright, it stops dead in its tracks. Upstream,
there's a colossal wall of water thirty feet high; and all that's
stopping it collapsing is that thundering loud bark."

"Whew!" Jack whistled, and Andy nodded and
winked.

"Like I said, I'm keeping an eye on that leery old ewe,
and Old Drumble's bark is so loud, the wax shoots out
of her ears. She takes off down the bank, the rest of the
mob following, and me running after them.

"We're galloping across the dried-up river-bed, one eye upstream in case that colossal wall of water collapses on us; Old Drumble's keeping up his thundering bark; the sheep are baa-ing; and I'm yelling to keep going or we'll all be drowned.

"A man's foot skids on something slippery, and I just have time to bend down and pick up several and stuff them down me shirt, and we're scrambling up the other bank, and running scared stiff but dry as a bone, up the road where it comes down to the ferry landing from Kopu.

"It's only when we're a couple of chains along the road that I realise I've lost me pipe," said Andy. "It must have fallen out of me gob as I yelled and ran across the river-bed."

"You said you picked up several things and stuffed them in your shirt," Jack told him. "Maybe you lost it when you bent down."

"I'll tell you about that in a minute," said Andy. "I'm looking round and patting me pockets, in case I've stuck me pipe away in one of them and, as I do so, Old Drumble stops his thundering bark.

"There's a spooky silence; the back of me neck goes cold, and there's a whispering sound — the rustle of wool standing up on the backs of all the sheep's necks."

They were passing Dunlops' place. Jack looked in,

hoping the Dunlop girls might notice him driving the sheep.

"The next moment," said Andy, "that colossal wall of water totters and collapses into a bellowing torrent of waves bucketing downstream between us and Old Drumble still on the other bank—"

"Ahhh!" The scream came from up the front of the mob. Jack stared and saw a man leap into the air, waving his arms and throwing himself back into Mrs Dickey's hedge.

Andy whistled, but Old Drumble was already taking charge, moving the front of the mob to the other side of the road.

"A swagger," said Andy. They followed the mob past the man who had half-buried himself in the eleagnus hedge.

Jack saw a thin-faced man in a broken felt hat, a broken old suit jacket, a collarless shirt with a stud stuck through the top buttonhole, baggy grey trousers fretted at the heels, and his bare feet stuck into broken grey sand-shoes without laces. In his arms, he clutched a sugarbag. Jack could see it didn't have a length of rope to make it into a proper swag, and the man didn't even seem to have a billy. His face was unshaven, and an old striped tie held up his trousers.

The swagger ignored Jack but looked nervously at Andy. "Don't suppose you know of any work going?"

116

he said, coming half out of the hedge then pressing back into it again, as Young Nugget trotted up for a closer look.

"Not round here. The factory's already got more men than they want." Andy took his time thinking. If anyone knew of a job going in the district, it would be Andy, Jack remembered his mother saying.

"I come through the Hinuera Valley last week, and there's some paddocks still closed up," said Andy. "They're a bit late getting in their hay this year because of the rain earlier. You might pick up a few days' work."

The broken-looking man looked down at his hands. Jack saw a scratch across the back of the right one, black with congealed blood that made the skin look white. Jack turned away.

"Do you know Hinuera?" Andy asked. Jack heard a shuffly noise and knew the man was shaking his head.

"Keep heading through Waharoa to Matamata. Bear south out of there, in that direction," Andy pointed, "and you can't miss it. Follow the signposts. Hinuera." He repeated it slowly. "You'll get there tomorrow and, with any luck, they'll be mowing their hay. They'll be in a hurry to get it in so, if you get taken on by the first cocky, you could go on from farm to farm for a week or so, as long as this weather lasts."

As he spoke, Andy was taking the jar of marmalade out of the pikau behind Nosy's saddle and handing it to the swagger who took it without a word, sliding it out of sight into his sugarbag.

"Here, you might as well have these," said Andy, and he took out the Bushells tea tin, and gave most of the biscuits to the swagger.

Mum's ginger-nuts, Jack thought. She wouldn't be too pleased with Andy giving them away.

"Keep bearing south through Matamata," repeated the man. The sound of his voice made Jack uncomfortable, so he looked away at the sheep, then glanced back.

The man was slipping a couple of ginger-nuts into the pocket of his jacket, and he put the others into the sugarbag with the same furtive gesture he'd used before. He shrunk away as Young Nugget came a bit closer, sniffing the biscuits.

"When you get to the factory," Andy gestured up Cemetery Road, "don't cross the railway lines, but follow the road to the right: you'll find yourself on the way to Matamata. Same thing when you get there: don't cross the lines, keep to the right of the F.A.C. building, and the road'll carry you past the district high school, Braeside Hospital, and clear of the town, then it'll cross the lines and you follow it. The Rotorua road goes off to the left, but you just keep going straight ahead. You'll see the A.A. sign for Hinuera."

"Keep going straight ahead," the swagger repeated. His eyes were a bit shifty, Jack thought. He didn't like him.

The swagger ducked his head and mumbled something. "And for the biscuits and jam," Jack heard. He felt like saying it wasn't jam but marmalade, but walked on, feeling the man's eyes on his back.

Down the road a bit, Andy said, "Might be an idea if you leave it to me to tell your mother what happened to her ginger-nuts, Jack, me boy. And me marmalade. At least I can return your mother's tin, but she's going to go butcher's hook when she finds out I've given away her jar."

Jack looked at him. "I felt sorry for the blighter," said Andy. "Those soft hands aren't going to get him a job on a hay paddock, not unless they're short of someone to lead the horse up and down.

"Townies, get them past the end of the tramlines, and they don't know how to look after themselves. Never had the chance to learn how, I suppose. And those towny clothes aren't going to be any use as the weather cools.

"Poor devil, didn't even find it easy saying thanks, and I can understand that. Out the monk under that hedge of Jim Dickey's, and he wakes to find half a dozen sheep standing over him. Probably thought they were going to eat him!" Andy chuckled, but Jack could hear something else in his voice.

"Old Drumble," he said, and he had to cough to clear his throat. "Andy, you said Old Drumble was still on the other bank of the Piako. At Pipiroa. How did he get across?"

"Now where was I up to? Something about that colossal wall of water collapsing, and looking for me pipe, and Old Drumble still on the other bank." Andy turned from looking back at the swagger making his way up the road towards the factory.

"How did Old Drumble get across the Piako?" His dry leathery brown face crumpled and creased and grinned at Jack.

"Where we just got across dry-footed, there's a torrent of dirty water thirty feet deep, and them huge waves bucketing downstream between us and Old Drumble on the other bank."

"How did he get across?" Jack asked again.

"I asks meself the very same question," said Andy. "How is that Old Drumble going to get across?"

Chapter Twenty

How Old Drumble Got Across the Flooded Piako, How He Made a Proper Pig of Himself at the Copper Maori, and Why He Couldn't Bark Again When They Got to Pipiroa With the Steers.

"No trouble to Old Drumble," said Andy. "He takes a deep breath, grabs hold of his nose with one paw, and dives head first into the flood."

"Did he get drowned?"

"Old Drumble's too cunning for that, Jack. He dog-paddles across under water — all them rough waves are just on the surface of the river, you see — comes to the top, scrambles up the bank our side, shakes himself and takes up the lead, and the sheep follow him towards Kopu.

"We stop up the road, once Old Drumble's dried out, light a fire, and fry half a dozen big flounder — that's what I picked up out of the dry river-bed and stuffed down me shirt. You see the water's tidal there, so the flatties come up on the incoming tide.

"'That wasn't a bad idea of yours,' I tell Old Drumble, 'holding the river up with your bark,' and he winks at me and helps himself to another flattie.

"A few days," said Andy to Jack, "and we've turned out them sheep on the new grass up the Tapu Valley. The cocky's that pleased to see them, he puts down a copper Maori for us: wild pork, kumaras, pumpkin, and spuds.

"Now pumpkin's one of Old Drumble's favourites, specially hangied. Come to think of it, if he's got a fault, it's that he's got no self-control at all, not when it comes to pumpkin out of a copper Maori.

"The only trouble with pumpkin," Andy told Jack, "it holds the heat. Many's the time I've warned the greedy old fool to give it time to cool but, no, he's got to get stuck into it, stuffing it down his gob with both paws before the cocky has time to uncover the rest of the hangi.

"Not only that, but the old guts is tearing into the pork. There's more wild pigs up the Tapu Valley than you could point a stick at. The cocky's put several weaners and a couple of fat maiden sows in the copper Maori, and Old Drumble's scoffing away, lips drawn back off his teeth, so he can rip into the pork without getting them burnt.

"Before the old coot's finished feeding his face, he's bright orange with pumpkin all over his coat, and greasy with pork fat from the tips of his ears to the white tuft on the tip of his tail. His table manners aren't the best; I know your mother wouldn't approve, Jack. In fact, you could say Old Drumble makes a right pig of himself.

"The cocky can't believe how much pumpkin Old Drumble puts away. He shoves his hat on to the back of his head and speaks in a slow sort of voice: I can still hear him.

"'I wouldn't of believed it,' he tells me, 'if I hadn't seen it with me own eyes!'

"We sleep off our big feed and, first thing next morning, we've got the steers moving on their way up to the Auckland sales. Old Drumble's burnt his throat, stuffing down all that hot pumpkin, so he's not going to be doing any barking in a hurry. I'm only surprised he didn't burn his paws, too, but they seem okay — at least, he's not limping any.

"You know," said Andy, "I'm riding Nosy behind the steers, and still finding it a bit hard to believe the way Old Drumble got the sheep across the Piako at Pipiroa. But it happened all right, I know."

"How did you know?" asked Jack.

"I know," said Andy, "because, as we're driving them steers down the Thames coast, my ears are still ringing from that thundering bark he used to stop the river. Nearly time for you to leave us, Jack."

"Tell us the rest of the story before we get to the cemetery?"

"Then we'd best take it easy." Andy whistled and, up ahead, Old Drumble slowed the mob.

"As we head towards Auckland," said Andy, "there's heavy rain all the way from Kopu, and a cloudburst up the Plains, Ngatea way, so the Piako's going to be carrying a fair bit of water, but we expect they'll have shifted the scow, so the ferry should be working and we can get the steers across.

"You wouldn't believe it, Jack, but we get the steers as far as Pipiroa, and they've dumped the sand over the side of the scow, but the flood's lifted and swung her hard in, and jammed her rubbing strake under the ferry's rubbing strake, what you call the belting. The noise is something dreadful, the two boats screeching, grinding, and tearing bits off each other. Nosy sticks her fingers in her ears; of course, a horse is fairly sensitive in the ear, as you know."

Jack nodded.

"The crew's just used the scow's punt to carry a hawser across the river, taken it round a big macrocarpa this side and made it fast; and they're going to try and winch the scow off the ferry, but they can't do it till the flood's gone down. It looks like we'll have to get the steers across the Piako ourselves, if we're going to get them up to Auckland in time for the sales. That cocky up the Tapu Valley, he's not going to be too pleased, if we don't get him a decent price because we're late."

"Did Old Drumble stop the river with his bark again?" Jack asked.

124

Andy shook his head. "I told you how he burnt his throat. The useless old coot's not going to be doing any barking for a couple of weeks.

"Not only that but, as we was bringing the steers down the coast, he disappears at Puru, north of Thames, and he doesn't show up again till we're coming past Totara Vineyards, several miles south of the town. I've just whipped into the vineyard and bought meself a bottle of Stanley Young Chan's port wine to rub on the inside of me throat for the rheumatism, when Old Drumble catches up with us, and he looks a proper shambles.

"Would you believe it, the wicked old sinner, he's done a pub crawl along Pohlen Street! Had a beer in every pub, he reckons, all eighty-six of them. Then he thinks for a while and croaks, 'No, I counted a hundred and twenty.'"

"A hundred and twenty pubs!" said Jack.

"He's lying!" said Andy. "There might have been a hundred and twenty pubs along Pohlen Street in the good old days when the Thames was flush with gold and kauri, but there's nothing like that number now. All the same, Old Drumble's had a skinful.

"Like I was saying, Jack, we gets to Pipiroa, and Old Drumble can't bark, and no wonder. Not just with scoffing hot pumpkin out of the hangi, and then tipping all that booze down his gullet. That's not all by a long shot. He's been smoking, too, and tobacco's harder on a dog's throat than hot pumpkin. Old Drumble's got no show of stopping the river with his bark."

"Did you swim the steers across?" Jack asked.

"That cloudburst up towards Ngatea," said Andy, "it's put the Piako over her banks, and the flood's bringing down rafts of raupo and flax, whole floating patches of swamp.

"A cream can bobs past, a couple of kerosene tins, and a strainer post with a few sprags of wire still stapled on; a cowshed with a miserable-looking cocky sitting on its roof and reading the *Weekly News* goes by on the flood, turning slowly and heading for the Hauraki Gulf; somebody's clothes-line sweeps down with its tea-tree prop and all the sheets and pillowslips still pegged on, and comes aground just below our feet.

"There's no show of swimming them steers across till the flood goes down, and by then we'll have missed the sales up in Auckland.

"'If you hadn't made a pig of yourself on hot pumpkin and tobacco,' I tells Old Drumble, 'you could have stopped the river with another thundering bark,' but he's not listening to a word I says.

"Instead, he climbs sort of gingerly down the bank and unpegs the sheets and pillowslips off the clothes-line. 'Give us a hand,' he croaks.'"

Andy nodded at Jack and said, "He rubs his sore throat and mouths at me, 'Tear them sheets and pillowslips into strips,' and he trots over to the steers and orders them to pay attention.

"His voice is that hoarse, he can't speak much above a whisper, but the steers can't look away. Well, you know what it's like when he puts his eye on you, eh?"

Jack nodded. "What did he say to the steers?"

"I can't hear what he's saying for the noise of the river," said Andy, "and those half-wild steers, they're pawing the ground and muttering; but, one by one, they drop their eyes before Old Drumble's terrible stare, turn their ears forward and listen."

Chapter Twenty-One

How Old Drumble Got His Balance
Out in Mid-Stream, How Andy Crossed the
Flooded Piako River Himself, and Why Jack
Felt Left Behind and All On His Own.

"OLD DRUMBLE TELLS THE STEERS what they've got to do," said Andy. "He shoves them into a long line, gives me the nod, and I go down it, blindfolding them with the torn-up strips of sheets and pillowslips. And, you know, they're so scared of his eye, they just stand and let me do it!"

"Mum says steers can be pretty dangerous," said Jack.

"They don't dare try nothing on," said Andy, "not with Old Drumble eyeing them."

"But how's he going to get them across the river blindfolded?"

"You're not going to believe this," said Andy.

"I'll believe it!"

"I told you about the hawser they've taken across the river to winch the scow off the ferry?" Jack nodded.

"The first steer picks up the tip of Old Drumble's tail between his teeth, the next one picks up that one's tail between his teeth, and so on down the line. Old Drumble takes the long tea-tree prop off the clothes-line between his choppers, gets it balanced, and steps out on the hawser like Blondin walking the tightrope over Niagara Falls. And, one by one, them blindfolded steers feel for the hawser with their feet and follow him out into mid-air."

"Heck!"

"I said you wouldn't believe me," Andy told Jack.

"I believe you!" In his mind, Jack was looking at the extraordinary sight of Old Drumble leading the blindfolded steers across the tightrope.

"Yeah, well I notice Old Drumble's taking good care not to look down: it's a fair sort of drop into the river and, if he goes, the steers go, too.

"It's not so bad for a man, of course, he's only got two feet to worry about, but a dog's got four: he's got to concentrate hard to keep them all on the tightrope."

"I never thought of—" Jack started to say.

"Think about it," Andy told him.

"Out in the middle, under the weight of them heavy steers, the hawser curves down towards the water. One end of Old Drumble's clothes-prop gets hooked in the branches of a gorse bush riding high on the flood. He takes one paw off the hawser, to get his balance, lifts another, and I yell to watch out, but me voice won't carry over the noise of the water.

"I see Old Drumble lift a third paw off the hawser. Just

for a moment, he's balancing on one foot, and scrabbling air with the other three. He's in big trouble, and there's nothing a man can do to help him. I holds me breath."

"What did he do?"

"I sees him take his fourth paw off the hawser!"

"True?"

"True as I'm telling you this, I see that remarkable dog take half a dozen steps through mid-air, find the hawser again with his first paw, then he puts down the second, the third, and the fourth, and he's got his balance. I lets out me breath, as he starts the long climb up the hawser to the opposite bank."

"What about the steers?"

"Oh, them? They just mooch along behind him, blindfolded and holding on to the tail of the one in front of them; they can't see anything, so why should they be worried?"

"Why should they be worried?" Jack repeated.

Andy called something to Young Nugget who gave a sharp bark. A handful of sheep rattled their dags and scampered after the rest.

"Next thing," said Andy, "I see Old Drumble hopping down on the bank the other side, dropping the prop from between his jaws, and whipping the blindfolds off the steers as they file past. One by one, they spit out the tail of the one in front and step on to solid ground."

"They all got across okay then?"

"The last one's still on the hawser when his blindfold slips; he thinks he's in mid-air, opens his mouth to give a shriek, and drops the tail of the steer in front of him."

"Did he drown?"

"Lucky for him, he's across and balancing on the hawser, just a couple of inches above the ground. He comes down a bit heavy-like, gets to his feet, and plunges bawling into the middle of the herd to escape Old Drumble's terrible eye."

"What about you, Andy? You're still on the other side."

"There's a crowd of local hicks on the far side; they cheered Old Drumble and the steers when they got across, but I can tell they're just waiting for me to make a fool of meself, trying to do a Blondin. Most of the jeering and jibing's coming from a no-good push of young larrikins who've got nothing better to do than to hang around waiting for a bit of cheap entertainment at my expense.

"I thinks to meself, 'I'll be a bit too cunning for them yahoos,' and I gives Old Drumble a whistle. He drops to it right off, picks up the tea-tree pole between his teeth, gets it balanced, and trots back along the hawser; he blindfolds me, and leads me across with the end of his tail in my mouth. I steps down on the road the other side of the Piako, take off the blindfold, and hand it to one of them young jokers.

"'How about giving it a go yourself?' I says to him, and

there's no more chiacking from his mates.

"But that one young joker I give the blindfold to, he's so embarrassed, he can't keep his trap shut, and he lets out with a 'Haw! Haw!' The next minute, Old Drumble's got him blindfolded, has the tip of his tail between the young joker's teeth, leads him across the other side, and trots back, leaving him there."

"Serves him right!" said Jack.

"Actually, I felt a bit sorry for him, no way back, and all his mates giving him a hard time. But Old Drumble's got the steers moving, and we're heading across the Plains for Waitakaruru."

"What happened to the young joker on the other side of the river?"

"He was too windy to try and walk the hawser on his own; he tramped to the Thames, worked his way up to Auckland on one of the mussel scows, and lit out for Australia. Best thing he could have done: his mates would have pointed the finger, never let him forget it.

"The grass came away good-oh after all that rain, so we took it easy, feeding and fattening the steers along the long acre all the way to Auckland, and arrived at the sales just in time to get the cocky the top price. You know, Jack, a lot of the skill in being a drover is in the timing."

"You did all right, then?" Jack said.

"I suppose you could say that."

"What was wrong?"

"Just that, getting across the Piako on the hawser like that, I didn't collect any flatties out of the river-bed, so we missed out on a feed that time."

Jack nodded. "Still . . . "

"Now, this," said Andy, "is about as far as your mother said you could go."

To Jack's astonishment, they were at the cemetery crossing already. On the main road, the other side of the railway lines, a lorry loaded with black sacks of basic slag slowed, took the turn-off, and disappeared between the barberry hedges that lined the road to Wardville.

Andy whistled, and Old Nell ran to the front of the mob and held them. Old Drumble ran back, offered Jack his paw to shake, and swapped places again with Old Nell.

Jack tried saying, "I'll just come over the crossing."

"'Not a foot on those lines,' I heard your mother say." Andy shook his head, until his hat and waistcoat creaked. "It'd be worth more than me life, if your mother found I'd encouraged you to disobey her and cross the lines." Andy gave a dry, leathery chuckle. "Besides, I'm not going to risk going without a feed of her ginger-nuts, next time I comes through Waharoa. We'll be seeing you, Jack."

Jack ran and climbed the cemetery gates. On top of one big, squared, white post, he stood and watched Old

133

Drumble look both ways up and down the railway lines, lead the mob across, and turn left on to the main road.

Old Drumble held the mob for a wagon to go by, then led them around the Wardville turn-off. His tail disappeared; the last of the mob vanished between the barberry hedges; Young Nugget, Old Nell, Andy, and Old Nosy disappeared.

On top of the post, Jack felt left behind, all on his own. He heard a crunch, and nearly fell off the post, looking around, expecting to see the sinister swagger.

"What are you staring at?" said a voice. "Hop on, or your mother will be taking our lunch off the table and giving it to the chooks."

Jack slid down, scrambled up on the bar, his father's arms around him, and felt safe.

Chapter Twenty-Two

Why You Don't Hang on to the Handlebars Too Hard, Why the Sheep Complained About Old Drumble Chewing Dark Havelock, and Why Jack's Voice Squeaked.

"DAD," JACK SAID, "did you know, Old Drumble's got a thundering loud bark?"

"He's a handy dog, Old Drumble, so he might have a bit of huntaway in him as well as border collie. Mostly, though, I've noticed he uses his eye and keeps his bark to himself." Jack's father steered the bike around a pothole.

"If you hang on to the handlebars too hard," he said, "you could have us both over. You'll take the skin off your knees; I'll take the knees out of my trousers; and that'll be the last time your mother lets you go droving with Andy.

"I've heard Old Drumble bark on occasion," he said, "a pretty dried-up sort of croak. Probably all the dust he's swallowed." Mr Jackman felt Jack loosen his excited grip on the handlebars and take a deep breath.

"Dad, Old Drumble burnt his throat eating hot

pumpkin straight out of a copper Maori, and he tried to cool it down by going on a pub crawl through Thames. He had a beer in every pub in Pohlen Street, all a hundred and twenty of them, and he smoked his head off, and that didn't help his throat one bit." Jack could hear his own voice racing.

"Old Drumble used to chew Havelock Dark Plug tobacco, because it said 'Aromatic' on the tin, but the sheep complained. They said Old Drumble's teeth turned yellow, and his breath wasn't all that aromatic either; they reckoned it stunk something rotten when he barked!"

"Did Andy tell you all this?" Jack's father asked.

"Yes, so it must be true." Jack looked at Mr Dickey's hedge. "We saw a swagger over there under the hedge. Wearing sand-shoes without any laces, and no belt — just a tie."

"Probably the same one I saw as I was leaving work. Poor devil, he looked down to it."

"Andy told him he might get a job haymaking up the Hinuera Valley."

Jack felt his father sigh. "Things are pretty tough," he said, "from one end of the country to the other. I waved down one of Stan Goosman's drivers and said he might give him a lift. I hope he did."

"Dad, why's that man a swagger?"

"There's lots who can't get jobs and take to the road,

trying to find work. Anyway, what's all this about Old Drumble chewing tobacco?"

"Andy said he started off smoking the tobacco instead of chewing it, but he couldn't grip the pipe properly. Dogs always have trouble with pipes because of their eye-teeth; so Old Drumble taught himself to roll the Havelock Dark, using raupo leaves for cigarette papers. He smoked it in all the Pohlen Street pubs, and Andy said that's no good for a dog's throat, specially not raupo leaves, 'cause they burn really hot."

Mr Jackman took his right hand off the handlebars and touched his hat to Mrs Dunlop, who was just coming out of her gate. Jack gripped tight again, but his father put his hand back down quickly, and Jack relaxed.

"Do you think Mum will let me help Andy drive the sheep along the Wardville road next time? Just as far as Griffiths' corner."

"That might be getting a bit far for me to pick you up and get you home in time for lunch. We'll have to see what we can arrange.

"I don't know that I'd go saying anything at home about Old Drumble's pub crawl: your mother's got a bit of a down on the booze and tobacco. She'll take a small glass of sweet sherry at a wedding breakfast or a twenty-first, but only for the toasts."

"I've seen her smoke," said Jack.

"That's different," said his father. "For years she kept a

packet of De Reszke ivory-tipped. On the side it said 'The aristocrat of cigarettes', so that was okay. She'd smoke one at Christmas and another on New Year's Day, 'just to be sociable'.

"Then Mrs Dainty caught her puffing a fag somebody had given her at the kitchen evening for the Toogood girl and told her that tobacco is a temptation of the Devil, so your mother gave it up for Lent, and never started again. I reckon you might be best keeping it to yourself, you know, about Old Drumble's Havelock Dark, and about the pubs, too."

"What's a temptation of the Devil, Dad?"

"Anything that Mrs Dainty disapproves of. But don't go saying that to your mother."

They bumped over the lines at the factory crossing, turned off the main road at the church corner, and Jack rang the bell as they went past the bottom end of Ward Street — just to show Harry Jitters and Minnie Mitchell. Then they were home, and he was so busy telling his mother about driving the mob all the way to the cemetery crossing, he didn't have time to tell her how Old Drumble stopped the Piako River.

But, after Mr Jackman had gone back to work, and they were doing the lunch dishes, Jack said to her, "We saw a swagger down near Dickeys' place, and Andy told him he might get a job up the Hinuera Valley. Dad saw him, too, and got him a lift on one of Stan Goosman's lorries."

"Mr Goosman to you, my boy. I suppose we've got to be thankful your father didn't bring him home for lunch."

"Why not?"

"You know perfectly well why not! And what else happened?"

Jack swallowed. "You're not going to believe this . . . "

"Leave that for me to decide." His mother's voice was crisp. "What sort of nonsense has Andy been filling you up with now?"

"It's not nonsense, Mum. True! Andy told me how Old Drumble barked so thunderously loud, he stopped the Piako River at the Pipiroa ferry, and they got the sheep across okay. Then Old Drumble stopped his thunderous bark, and the river ran again."

His mother pressed her lips together. "Stopping the Piako River?" she said. "It sounds remarkably like the story of the time that Moses parted the Red Sea to let the children of Israel escape from the Egyptians. That Andy had better watch out what he's saying." She shook her head.

"If that man thinks he's going to go repeating Bible stories and passing them off as his own yarns, Mrs Dainty will put the vicar on to him."

"Andy stuffed his shirt full of flatties as they crossed the dry river-bed," Jack said, "and they lit a fire down the road and cooked up a feed in the frying pan."

His mother pulled out the plug, watched the dishwater circle and disappear with a gurgle, wiped around the sink, and sniffed. "Parting the Piako River, indeed. And filling his shirt with smelly fish. And then what?" She wrung the dishcloth so hard that Jack felt his throat.

Carefully, he dried the knives and forks one by one, because his mother always said you can't dry them properly if you just pick up a handful. He put them in their drawer one by one, too, just in case. Jack didn't want Mrs Dainty sooling the vicar on to Andy.

"And up the Tapu Valley," he heard himself gabbling, "where they took the sheep, the farmer put down a copper Maori for them, and Old Drumble scoffed down so much hot pumpkin the cocky said he wouldn't have believed it, if he hadn't seen it with his own eyes."

"I'd have to see it with mine, too, before I'd believe a word of it," said Jack's mother.

"He loves pumpkin done in a hangi, Old Drumble." His voice raced away on its own again. "Andy reckons he can't get enough of it. That was the trouble: he hoed into it with both paws, shoving it down his gob without waiting for it to cool; that's how he burnt his throat."

"Oh, yes?"

"True, Mum. Andy said so." His voice jabbered higher and faster. "Old Drumble's throat felt as if it was on fire, so he ran all the way into the Thames and did a pub crawl along Pohlen Street, drinking beer in every single

140

one, to cool it down. A hundred and twenty pubs; that's a hundred and twenty beers — and they weren't just handles, they were schooners. Andy reckons that's a fair bit for a dog to put away."

"Indeed!"

Encouraged, Jack looked up, saw his mother was staring at him, and plunged on. "And he smoked his head off, Havelock Dark plug tobacco rolled in raupo leaves. A smoke with every beer, and a beer in every pub.

"Andy says that's the worst thing you can do to a dog's bark, encourage him to take up smoking. Jeez! I wish I'd been there, with Old Drumble, doing his pub crawl . . . " Jack's voice tailed off, as he felt his mother's eye glitter cold.

"What — did — you — say — John — Jackman?" Her voice was slow, each word separate from the next. "Taking the Lord's name in vain! Are my ears deceiving me? Did I hear you aright, that you've taken up drinking and smoking?"

"I was just telling you what Old Drumble did," Jack squeaked.

Chapter Twenty-Three

Rolling Home Blaspheming, Swearing,
and Reeking of Beer and Tobacco,
Why Jack Glanced at the Kitchen Window,
and Why His Mother Shook Her Apron
and Laughed Helplessly.

"THE IDEA! I let you and your father out of my sight for a few minutes and, in no time, the pair of you are rolling home blaspheming, swearing, and reeking of beer and tobacco!

"Next thing, he'll be taking you over to the billiard saloon, and teaching you to gamble with the bookie. What's the world coming to, I'd like to know?"

"It wasn't Dad's fault, Mum! It was Old Drumble who went on a pub crawl through the Thames."

"That's right: blame it on an innocent dog. I think you'd better get out and mow the back lawn. And don't you dare go thinking for a moment that you're a dog who frequents billiard saloons, and swears, and drinks beer, and smokes tobacco!"

"But, Mum—"

"No buts! If I hear so much as a single bark, you'll be in trouble. Copper Maoris, pub crawls, chewing tobacco.

142

I suppose I should be grateful they haven't taught you to spit!

"And parting the river to get the sheep across . . . What sort of pagan rubbish is that old Andy going to come up with next?" demanded Mrs Jackman. "The idea of it!"

"But—" Jack tried to say.

"I thought I said 'No buts'? Standing there with your mouth wide open, gawping at me like a ninny. I suppose you're waiting for me to cut the grass for you? Hang up that tea towel properly, and get out there and start mowing that lawn, at once. And, if you know what's good for you, Jack Jackman, you won't even dare think of going near any of those dirty hotels! Thank heavens we live in a dry district."

The grass was long, the lawn mower a heavy pig of a thing to push. What made it even harder was that his mother came to the back door and called, "What's the use of mowing the lawn if you don't use the catcher?

"I don't want grass clippings tracked in all over my lino. You put the catcher on at once, and you can rake the bit you've already cut. Get the wheelbarrow, and make sure you put the clippings on your father's compost — and don't you dare bark at me, Jack Jackman!"

"I wasn't barking, Mum. True—"

"I wouldn't even think of it," his mother warned. "Not if you value your life . . . "

Jack raked up the grass, put it in the wheelbarrow, and tried to run it up a plank and tip it on top of the compost heap.

It always looked good fun, when Dad did it, but Jack's legs and arms weren't long enough, so he tried running up the plank behind the wheelbarrow himself. The iron wheel slipped, the plank tipped sideways, and Jack fell off the compost heap. First, the clippings came down on top of him, then the heavy wooden wheelbarrow, then the plank.

He got to his feet, spitting grass. "Pig!" he told the plank and propped it back in place. "Pig!" he told the wheelbarrow, and stood it up the right way. "Pig!" he told the clippings, as he raked them up and threw them on the compost heap. "Pig-swine!" he hissed at them all: the compost heap, the plank, the wheelbarrow, and the clippings.

He hooked the wire eyes of the catcher over the lugs on the lawn mower, took up the handle and shoved. The catcher soon filled with grass, the mower was twice as heavy to push, then it stopped because of a cabbage tree leaf that got itself wound around the axle.

"Pig-shit!" Jack told it, then felt all hot, and glanced at the kitchen window. Had the curtain moved? With her strong eye and ears, his mother could tell what he was thinking through the door; she'd have no trouble hearing him swear through the glass. And, just at that moment,

Harry Jitters came swaggering, whistling, waving his arms, and driving an imaginary mob of sheep up Ward Street.

Jack growled deep in his chest as Harry put his mob across the Turangaomoana Road — without even looking out for traffic. Clumsily, he drove them past the hall on to the grass, left them grazing under the eyes of his invisible dogs, and turned to walk back. Jack's heart dropped as he realised that Harry was coming to stare and sneer, to chiack him like Andy's yahoo at the Pipiroa ferry. For a moment, black despair filled his heart, then an idea came into his head.

Jack dropped the lawn mower handle, stood back, and looked at the strip he'd just mown. He put his head on one side, pursed his lips, knelt down, and brushed his hand over the cut grass. He stood up, emptied the catcher, pushed the mower the length of the lawn, and went through the same act. It felt a bit silly, kneeling, brushing the grass, putting his head on one side, but he cut another strip, knelt, and put his head on one side a third time. When he stood up, he backed over towards the fence, looked at the cut lawn, and whistled in admiration at his own work. "Whew!"

"We know what you're up to, Jack Jackman," said a loud voice behind him.

"Where'd you spring from?" Jack didn't wait for a reply, but crouched and studied the lawn again.

"Haw! Haw! Haw!" Harry Jitters mocked. Jack ignored him.

"We know what ya game is, Jack Jackman."

"Yeah?" Jack tried to sound nonchalant.

"Yeah! Tryin' to make it look like fun, mowin' your lawn. An' we know where you pinched the idea from, too."

"What idea?"

"That idea. The one outta that book Mr Strap read to us."

"What book?"

"The one about Tom Sawyer whitewashin' his aunt's fence. That's where ya pinched the idea from."

"I did not!"

"Haw! Haw! Haw! You don't fool me, Jack Jackman. It's hard work, pushin' that heavy old mower of yours, specially with the catcher. And you're not going to get me doin' any mowin', not even if you give me a bag of marbles, and an old rat and a string to swing it with. So there!"

Jack ignored Harry, pushed the mower another length of the lawn, took off the catcher, and carried it across to dump the clippings on the compost heap. It was unfortunate that — just as Jack heaved up the catcher — Harry barked. Jack's hands did something wrong, the catcher tipped too soon, and half the clippings went on the ground.

The kitchen window popped open. "You pick up those clippings and put them on the compost heap at once," said the voice of doom. Harry Jitters heard it, and kept still and silent.

Jack picked up the clippings, and looked at how much still remained to be mown. He'd be there all day. "It's not fair," he said aloud. Harry Jitters heard it and couldn't help himself. He stuck his head right through the fence, shoving hard to get his ears between the wires, and barked again but, this time, it was Harry's rowdiest huntaway bark, loud and insistent — "Wow! Wow! Wow!" — his head jerked up and down. "Wow! Wow! Wow!"

"I'll teach you to come barking around my house!" Mrs Jackman burst out the front door, charged down the steps, flung open the gate, and nearly caught Harry, whose head was stuck between the wires. He jerked it free and ran, yelling with fright and pain, the backs of his ears scratched — "Ow! Ow! Ow!" — back down to his own end of Ward Street. Jack's mother stood, shaking her apron after him, laughing helplessly.

"Who said you could stop work?" she asked Jack, who'd run out and stood beside her, barking after Harry. "A drunkard in the family. Smoking tobacco, blaspheming, swearing — and gambling, too, I've no doubt. You get on with your lawn."

But there was no anger in her voice, and she'd laughed at Harry. Jack just had to tell her the rest of the story.

"And, Mum," he said, "coming back, they were driving a mob of steers up to the sales in Auckland, and the Piako was in flood at Pipiroa, and Old Drumble blindfolded the steers and made them walk a tightrope across the river, holding their tails in each other's mouths. And he had to blindfold Andy and stick the end of his tail in his mouth to get him across, too. And he got the steers up to Auckland in time to get the top price."

"I'm pleased to hear it," said his mother. "Now, if you're not cutting that grass by the time I've counted to ten, I'll stick your tail in your mouth and give you the end of a rope around your legs, my boy. One, two, three . . . "

Whirr! Whirr! Whirr! Jack shoved the lawn mower hard at a patch of rye grass that just bent and wouldn't cut properly. He guessed now wasn't the best time to ask his mother if he could help drive the next mob out on the Wardville road.

Chapter Twenty-Four

Why Harry Jitters Stopped and Barked from the Corner, Why Mrs Dainty Suddenly Felt Much Better, and How Mr Strap Said the Maoris Got Here from Hawaiki.

LITTLE BY LITTLE, the continent of long grass shrunk to an island and, as it grew smaller, it took longer to cut, because Jack had forgotten what he was supposed to be doing.

He'd begun by pushing the mower fast, but that was too hard, and it didn't cut well. So he tried pushing it slow, but that didn't cut well either. Specially not the rye grass, which just bent over whether he was pushing the mower fast or slow.

Jack looked at the kitchen window and whispered, "Bloody old rye grass!" Slower and slower he pushed. Slower still. And still slower.

If it was too far for Dad to pick him up on the bike, from out Griffiths' corner, maybe he could get a lift back to Waharoa with one of the carriers, he thought to himself.

After picking up the cream in the morning, the carriers spent the rest of the day carting bags of manure, rolls of barbed wire, and timber between the railway station and the farms. Andy would get one of them to give him a lift home.

As Jack thought of that, the mower blades slowed till they stopped. He leaned against the handle as if still pushing, but his feet stopped moving, and he looked at the remaining long grass. There seemed to be more of it than ever. It wasn't fair.

"Looking at it won't cut so much as a single blade of grass!" He leapt in the air. "You can just mow all that side again!" said his mother's voice. "If a job's worth doing, it's worth doing well. Put some elbow grease into it!"

"Mum?" Jack begged.

"What do you want now?"

"Mum, when you were a little girl, did your mother make you mow the lawns?"

"When I was a little girl, we didn't have a mower, so I had to learn to use a scythe. Children had it hard in those days. Don't think you can go asking me questions and use that as an excuse to stop mowing. Get on with it, or the grass is going to need cutting again before you've finished."

Whirr! Whirr! Whirr! Jack had already found that pushing the mower fast meant it didn't cut the rye grass. You had to push it just right, not too fast, not too slow and, even then, you were lucky if it cut properly. Jack's gloom deepened.

Harry Jitters sneaked back along Ward Street, grinning nervously, and hid in the bamboo patch. He was wondering if he dared tear past Jack's place, barking as he ran. If he really went for it, he should be around the corner and out of sight before Jack's mum came after him.

Harry felt the scratches on the backs of his ears and thought of how she'd nearly caught him yelling and trying to get his head out of the fence. Mrs Jackman could move! It might be safer just to give a bark from behind the bamboos.

Harry put up his head, barked once, thought he heard Mrs Jackman coming, and skedaddled whimpering, but at Whites' corner, he saw Minnie Mitchell watching him from outside her gate. He looked over his shoulder, pulled up, turned himself into a huntaway, and gave a fair volley, "Wow! Wow! Wow!" towards the bottom end of Ward Street.

Even if it was too far for Mrs Jackman to hear, it sounded pretty good; besides, when Minnie saw the blood on the backs of his ears, she'd know how brave he was.

At the other end of Ward Street, Jack emptied the catcher for the last time, and sniffed the smells of fresh-cut grass and compost.

"What's that boy dreaming about now?" his mother said to herself and opened the window. "Put the mower away," she called. "Hang up the catcher, and see you close the shed door. Then you can run along the street and play with Harry for a while, but see that you keep an eye out for your father, and come home with him."

Jack pulled his lips back off his teeth and growled as he ran down Ward Street to get his own back on Harry Jitters. He wasn't going to be an eye dog this time, nor a huntaway: he was going to be a pig dog, a holder, with a bit of bully in him.

Holders with a bit of bully in them hang on and don't let go. They can't even bark much because their nose is jammed hard up against the pig, where they're hanging on to its cheek or ear. But they growl, deep in their chest. "Grrr!" Jack said.

Teeth fastened in the gristle of its cheek, nose hard up against its jaw, laying his own body back along the boar's side, so it couldn't hook him with its tusks, Jack growled again, "Grrrr! Grrrr!" so that Mrs Dainty walking home from the shops with her basket said, "I hope you're not making that noise at me, Jack Jackman!"

"Hello, Mrs Dainty," said the holder, turning himself into a boy.

"I said, I hope you're not making that noise at me."

"No, Mrs Dainty. I'm growling at Harry Jitters, because he barked at me."

"You mustn't make up fibs, or I'll tell your mother. Harry Jitters isn't even here. I saw him running home, as

I came round the corner from the butcher's."

Jack stared back and was silent. It was never any use trying to explain to Mrs Dainty.

"That's how it always starts, with a little fib. Then whoppers. And the next thing is, you're telling lies. And we all know where that leads. The gallows!"

Mrs Dainty pursed her mouth. She'd been a bit down to it, that morning, not sure whether to go and collect her mail and do her bit of shopping, because she was afraid of being chased by a bull every time she put her nose outside her gate. It wasn't right: all these mobs of wild animals being driven along the street. But now, suddenly, she felt much better. She swung her basket and walked on briskly.

Jack growled under his breath, and made a quick Unga-Yunga face after her. He would have stuck out his tongue and tried his puku dance, but everyone knew Mrs Dainty always spun around, to try and catch you being rude behind her back.

Mrs Dainty did spin around, but Jack was already trotting down Ward Street towards Harry and Minnie, who stood outside their gates, watching him coming. Harry moved over and stood closer to Minnie.

"Your mother took the skin off the back of poor Harry's ears," Minnie told Jack.

"She did not! He stuck his head through the fence, barking at me, and he couldn't pull it out fast enough when Mum charged outside and nearly caught him, and then he got his ears tangled up in the wires. Serves him right for having such big lugs!"

But Minnie Mitchell was not beaten easily. "Where were you going this morning?" she asked. "With that dirty old man, and that dirty old dog trotting in front, and all those dirty old sheep?"

"Andy," said Jack, "is the best drover, and Old Drumble's the best leading dog in the southern hemisphere. We took the mob down through Waitoa and Ngatea, and had a bit of trouble getting them across the Piako River at the Pipiroa ferry."

Minnie was too smart to be caught, but Harry fell for it. "Where's the Pipiroa ferry?" he asked, touching the backs of his ears delicately and examining his fingertips for blood.

"The creek behind the factory," said Jack, "it runs down the back of Dickey's place and the pig farm, behind the pa, under the road to Walton, and turns itself into the Waitoa River, and then it becomes the Piako and runs into the Firth of Thames and the Hauraki Gulf, and then it goes up the Pacific, over the equator and the North Pole and down the Atlantic, down over the equator and the South Atlantic and the South Pole and comes up and turns left and comes up the back of Waharoa again." Jack took a breath. "Andy and Old Drumble, they've driven sheep that way lots of times. It's the same way

154

the Maoris came to New Zealand from Hawaiki in their Great Fleet."

"Aw . . . " Harry said, uncertainly.

"You think you're smart, don't you, Jack Jackman!" said Minnie Mitchell. She wasn't sure about the equator and the North and South Poles, but Mr Strap had told them about the Maoris coming to New Zealand from Hawaiki in a fleet of canoes, and there'd been something about it in the *School Journal*. She picked at the left shoulder of her dress with her right hand, so the puffed sleeve stood out as it was supposed to. "Anyway, how did they get the sheep over all that sea?"

"Easy," Jack said. "Old Drumble can do anything."

Chapter Twenty-Five

Where Old Drumble Tied the Ends
of the Tightrope, Keeping Out of the Way
of the Interfering Old Biddy, and
Why Jack Yelped and Looked Across
the Paddocks Towards Waharoa.

JACK LOOKED SCORNFULLY at Minnie Mitchell and Harry Jitters. "How did Old Drumble get the sheep across the sea?" he repeated.

"He made the sheep hold each other's tails in their mouths, and blindfolded them, and led them along a tightrope. And Andy followed them with Old Nell and Young Nugget and Nosy holding each other's tails in their mouths. All the way up the Pacific, over the North Pole, down the Atlantic, over the South Pole, and back up to Waharoa." Jack took another breath.

"You're silly, Jack Jackman." Minnie plucked at her puffed right sleeve with her left hand and smiled at one shoulder, then the other. "Don't take any notice of his stories."

"Did Old Drumble wear a blindfold?" Harry asked.

"Course not! He was out in front, leading, so he held Andy's stick in his mouth and balanced like Blondin walking across Niagara Falls. Old Drumble's got a good eye and perfect balance."

"Is that true?"

"Course it's true!"

"It is not true!" Minnie lifted the hair behind her ears with both hands, tucked it back in place, and patted it. "He's just making it up. Anyway, where'd they tie the ends of the rope?" She shifted her red belt, so the buckle was in the exact middle of her waist.

"Old Drumble tied the rope between the North Pole and the South Pole. And when they came to the equator, he led them along it."

"The equator isn't a rope!"

"It is so. You look at the big map at school, and you can see it. Remember, Mr Strap said it's a long line right around the world."

"All the same," said Minnie, "the Maoris came the other way, not round the middle of the world," but Harry didn't understand what she meant. Her voice brightened, and she plucked to show off her puffed sleeves again. "Hello, Mr Jackman!" she said.

"Hello, Minnie! Hello, Harry! Jump on, and I'll give you a lift home."

Jack scrambled up on the bar, leaned out around his father's arm, and yelled back, "And next time I'm going to help them drive all the way out the Wardville road, as far as Griffiths' corner."

"Don't go getting your hopes too high," said his father, "but I might just have a lift jacked up for you. The county council's going to be carting shingle from out the Gordon, and they'll be running backwards and forwards for the next couple of weeks; so Bob Murdoch told me. With a bit of luck, we should be able to get you a lift back into Waharoa with him, next time Andy comes through."

"Corker!"

"It's not for sure yet; we'll have to see how it works out, and if your mother approves, of course. Now, what've you been up to this morning?"

"I had to mow the back lawn."

"Good! That saves me from doing it. What happened?"

"I told Mum about Old Drumble burning his throat on hot pumpkin, and going on a pub crawl."

"What else did you tell her?"

"I said 'Jeez!' and Mum said I was taking the name of the Lord in vain, and she said she wasn't having the pair of us reeling home drunk, smoking tobacco, and swearing. And something else. Bla—something."

"Blaspheming?"

"That's it."

"Sounds like the sawdust heap again . . . " The bike paused at the corner of Whites' Road. "I told you to keep it to yourself, all that business about hot pumpkin, and Old Drumble going on a pub crawl."

"I couldn't help it. Mum just looks at me, and I have to tell her everything. It's her strong eye. She said it's a wonder you haven't taught me how to spit and put bets on with the bookie."

"I suppose I'll have to take my punishment." Mr Jackman pedalled on towards home, but Jack had heard him say that before, so he just grinned to himself.

"Remember," his father said, "how you got yourself into trouble, telling your mother about her strong eye?"

"Dad, Mum can tell what I'm thinking through a closed door. And when she stares at me, it's just like the time Old Drumble eyed me. She's got strong ears, too."

"I know." His father sounded sympathetic. "Even when I hammered my thumb, the other day, I didn't swear, in case she heard. Try to remember not to mention her ears."

"I didn't say anything about them today. Are you really going to take me over to the billiard saloon and teach me how to put bets on with the bookie, Dad?"

"Do you want to get me hung! You go talking like that, your mother'll sool Mrs Dainty on to me."

"But Mum said you were going to teach me how to gamble."

"I don't think that's what she meant."

"And I got into trouble with Mrs Dainty. She thought I was going 'Grrr!' at her, but I told her I was just being a holding dog."

"And did she believe you?"

"She never believes anybody. That's why I pulled a face."

"Did she catch you?"

"No, but she said I'd started off fibbing and I'd finish up on the gallows. What are the gallows, Dad?"

"The interfering old biddy! Keep out of her way's the best thing."

"The trouble is she sneaks up and listens to what I'm thinking. She must have strong ears, too."

"Now," said Mr Jackman, bumping the gate open with the front wheel, "when we get inside, nothing about your mother's eye and ears. And keep off Mrs Dainty's too. What do you reckon Mum's got for our tea?"

"I hope it's mince. I love mince! Sausages best of all, then mince with mashed potatoes. So I can make rivers through the spuds."

"I used to like doing that, too, till your mother stopped me."

Jack kept off his mother's strong eye and ears and Mrs Dainty's, too. He went the other way, when he saw Mrs Dainty coming. He got the spade and trimmed the edges around the lawn without being told, tried to behave himself, and things went quietly; then at last the day came when he helped drive a mob with Old Drumble and Andy all the way out to Griffiths's corner on the Wardville road.

"Just hang around at the corner. Bob Murdoch will be keeping an eye out for you," his father had told him.

Now Andy said, "Here we are, Jack. As far as the big poplar on the corner, and not a step further. Those were your Mum's words."

Jack shook hands with Old Drumble and patted Nosy. He nodded, winked, clicked, and said hooray to Andy, and watched them head along the road, past the row of lawsonianas that marked Middletons' place, heading towards the turn-off to Te Aroha.

"Next time," Jack said to himself, "I'll ask if I can go as far as the Te Aroha turn-off." He didn't know the road beyond the turn-off, so it sounded mysterious and he repeated it aloud a couple of times. "The turn-off to Te Aroha . . . The Te Aroha turn-off . . . " Jack decided he preferred "The Te Aroha turn-off."

"You see you wait there, by the big poplar with the eleagnus growing over it," his mother had said. "Don't you dare take as much as a single step beyond the corner. Don't run out on the road. And don't go climbing the poplar. Just wait there till Mr Murdoch picks you up, and don't forget to thank him."

Jack stood on the corner, and watched a sparrow fly into the poplar high above the eleagnus. It was getting late in the summer, but spabs nested several times. Then he saw it: a nest so high that the wind bent the branch over until the untidy mass of dead grass and straw woven among the twigs lay on its side. Jack thought of the eggs inside the pocket lined with soft down, in the middle of the nest.

It wouldn't take long to shin up and stick his hand inside, to see if there were any eggs, but what if Mr Murdoch came along while he was up the tree? He'd drive on and tell his father he wasn't there. His father would bike home and tell his mother. And she'd come running out to Griffiths' corner and teach Jack a lesson . . .

Jack looked up the road. The mob had disappeared past Middletons' lawsonianas. He stretched out his left leg in the direction they'd gone, and held the foot a couple of inches above the ground. That wasn't taking a step past the corner. Not so long as his foot didn't touch. He pulled back his left foot, put his weight on that leg, and stretched out his right foot and held it just above the ground.

Perhaps his left leg wasn't used to holding his right foot out. After all, he was right-handed, and maybe feet are the same, and his left leg wasn't as strong as his right. Perhaps he lost his balance. Perhaps a gust of wind blew him over. Jack's face screwed up, and he gave a yelp and looked across the paddocks towards Waharoa, as he realised that he had taken a step too far.

Chapter Twenty-Six

Cannibal Swaggers Crawling Along the Drain,
Why Andy Grew Mint in Old Drumble's
Kennel, and Why Old Drumble Climbed on
the Roof and Sniffed the Smoke.

JACK PULLED BACK THE FOOT that had taken a step too far, turned, and bolted towards home. He stopped, crept back to the corner, and stood on the same spot — he knew exactly where he'd stood before because of a whitey bit of stone.

Jack looked past Middletons' lawsonianas towards the bend where the mob had disappeared, and thought he saw something move. He yelped again. What if it was a cannibal swagger coming to punish him for taking a step too far?

After Jack had told Harry and Minnie about the swagger down Cemetery Road, Harry told his mother, and she warned him that swaggers eat little boys. Mrs Jackman told Jack that was nonsense, and he had believed her — but now he wasn't so sure.

He looked again, and saw the road was empty, but he was sure he'd seen something move. He looked at the deep drain beside the road, one of that network of drains his father had described to him, which finished up running into the Waihou River.

The drain was overgrown. A hungry swagger could creep along it, and you'd never see him till he leapt out. Jack thought of Andy. He'd have seen any swagger and sent back Old Drumble to make sure Jack was safe, specially if it was a hungry-looking swagger.

He looked again, and made sure the road was empty. There was water running in the bottom of the drain, so he'd hear any swagger splashing along it. Still, he said to himself, he'd stick to the middle of the road, just to be safe.

Jack stood on his right foot on the same whitey-looking bit of stone and stretched out his left foot, then his right foot, then his left again. This time, it was his left foot which touched the ground.

He didn't yelp and run this time. He looked but couldn't see the cannibal swagger coming. He peered into the drain. Nothing happened. He took another step. Nothing happened, and Jack took another step. By the time the lorry came around the distant bend, he was a couple of chains down the road. He bolted back and waited on the corner, not putting his weight on his left foot.

Mr Murdoch pulled up beside him. "Hop aboard," he said. "I saw Andy and Old Drumble up the road, heading towards the Te Aroha turn-off."

"I helped them drive the mob here, but Mum said it's as much as my life's worth to take a step past the corner."

Mr Murdoch nodded as if he understood. "That door needs a good slam to shut it properly. That's it." He let in the clutch, and Jack felt the lorry drag itself slowly along the road.

"So you reckon you're going to become a drover?" Mr Murdoch shouted over the engine.

"Mum says I can just put it out of my mind; Dad says to wait and see. He says it might seem okay now but, if I had to walk for a few hours in wet clothes, I might see it differently. Still, I like listening to Andy's stories, and watching Old Drumble leading. Why are we sort of dragging, Mr Murdoch?"

"That's the weight of the shingle you're feeling through the back of the seat. It makes a heavy load. Why were you hopping on one foot, when I picked you up, Jack?"

"I got a prickle."

"Better a prickle than a stone-bruise. Here's the factory crossing, and there's your old man, waiting to give you a dub home. Hooray, Jack!"

"Thanks, Bob," his father called. "I've had a word with Dines Barker about those trees of his. I'll be getting on to the firewood soon, and I'll let you know.

"That worked out well," he said to Jack. "We're going to be in good time for lunch. Did Andy tell you anything more about Old Drumble hitting the bottle?"

"Not hitting the bottle, but he told me about the time Old Drumble was really belting the hops along. It all came of Andy giving Old Drumble an empty whisky barrel for a kennel. They were having a spell off the road and, after sleeping in the barrel a few nights, Andy said Old Drumble was so cross-eyed, he couldn't face down a newborn lamb. Andy said that whisky barrel was his downfall. I got a prickle in my foot, Dad."

"Remind me, when we get home. What did Andy do about the barrel?"

"They swapped," Jack told his father. "Old Drumble slept in Andy's bunk, and Andy slept in the barrel himself, for a couple of nights, but it didn't do anything for him. He said he sniffed hard, but he couldn't smell a trace of whisky, just Old Drumble's stink."

"Perhaps Old Drumble licked the inside of the barrel?"

"I said that, but Andy said he'd licked it inside and out, himself, before he made it into a kennel. He thought it could be that Old Drumble has a powerful imagination, and he talked himself into getting drunk each night, after he'd gone to bed. Andy reckons Old Drumble has such powerful dreams," said Jack, "half the time he wakes himself barking."

"I've known dogs growl in their sleep," his father nodded. "I always wonder if they're scared of ghosts."

"Well, one morning," said Jack, "Old Drumble couldn't stand straight, after a night in the whisky barrel. That's when Andy said he really looked as if he'd been belting the hops along and decided he'd better do something about it, or he'd have an alky on his hands.

"Mint likes a damp spot, Andy said, and the guttering by the back door had rusted through, so he stood Old Drumble's kennel on end, filled it with dirt, and planted a root of mint that Mum gave him."

Jack was so busy, telling his father the story of the whisky barrel, he didn't notice Harry Jitters and Minnie Mitchell standing outside their gates. Mr Jackman smiled at them, but Jack stared straight over the front wheel, chattering on.

"The mint came away good-oh, but the first lot Andy picked, he threw into the billy with his spuds, and they came out tasting of whisky. Andy says he likes a drop of the hard stuff as much as anyone, but not with new potatoes."

Harry Jitters heard something about whisky and new potatoes and stared, mouth wide open, but Minnie smiled back. "Hello, Mr Jackman," she cried and shook her curls.

"It was like Jack didn't even see us!" Harry said to her. "He just went on jabbering to his father."

"If you've got nothing worth saying, why don't you

close your mouth!" Minnie told him. She flounced through her gate, and slammed it so the latch clashed, leaving Harry open-mouthed.

He took a step after Minnie, but she was away up the path, tossing her curls and shrugging. Harry turned and stared after Mr Jackman's bike, and didn't know what to do, so he stuck his head in the air and barked.

It was his noisiest huntaway bark and went on and on, till the bike had crossed Whites' Road. Then Harry stopped barking and ran after, as far as the corner, where he stood and barked towards the bottom end of Ward Street, "Wow! Wow! Wow!"

Jack didn't notice the huntaway barking, because he was telling his father the rest of his story about Old Drumble's alcoholic kennel.

"That's when Andy knocked the bands off the barrel and split the staves apart for kindling wood," he told his father. "And, he said, it was the best kindling ever! It lit, no trouble, and burnt with a blue flame that must have come from the whisky, and Old Drumble climbed on the roof of Andy's whare, and sniffed the smoke coming out of the chimney, and got half-cut, just on the smell. Andy said he fell off the roof, crawled under the Christmas plum tree, and slept it off."

"I'm glad you told that story to me," said Mr Jackman, "and not your mother. Now, remember, not a word about the whisky barrel and Old Drumble. And I wouldn't go saying 'half-cut' to her. It's the sort of language that gets her going, if you see what I mean."

Jack felt him nod and wink, and hung on to the handlebars as the front wheel bumped the gate open. Even though his father couldn't see, he nodded and winked back, as they went around the side of the house.

"The trouble is . . . " he said, as he slipped off the bar and rubbed his behind, while his father took the bicycle clips off the cuffs of his trousers, "the trouble is I always mean not to say anything to Mum, but she puts her strong eye on me, and I hear myself jabbering away."

"She has that effect on me, too," said his father. "Try telling her a different story. Andy must have told you some others."

"I'll try. But it's her eye."

"I know," said Mr Jackman.

Chapter Twenty-Seven

Why Jack Got the Prickle in His Foot, the Ancient Maori Myth of Tai Taylor, and How the Bull Waited for the Kids, Frothing and Bellowing Outside the School Gate.

"SOMETIMES I HEAR MY VOICE gabbling away, nineteen to the dozen, telling Mum a story, just making it up as it goes. Will you squeeze the prickle out of my foot?"

"As long as lunch isn't on the table, waiting for us."

"Dad, when are you going to cut the firewood out at Mr Barker's place? Can I come and help?"

"I'm depending on you for a hand," his father said, and Jack smiled. "Now, remember what I said about Old Drumble and the whisky barrel. Hello, dear, I'm just going to dig out a prickle."

His mother stared as Jack hopped in the door. "You didn't put that foot to the ground past Griffiths's corner?" she asked.

Jack looked away.

"It's no good pretending to me, I can see it written all over your face. You went beyond the corner, John Jackman! Didn't you? Come on, own up!"

"Just a step."

"How many just a steps?"

"Just a few."

"How many just a few?"

"Just a couple of yards."

"How many just a couple of yards?"

"Just to the next telegraph post."

"That's a chain — twenty-two yards. How many telegraph posts?"

"Just a few."

"I said how many just a few telegraph posts?"

"Just a couple. Then I saw Mr Murdoch coming, and I turned and ran back to Griffiths' corner."

"Griffiths's corner. How often do I have to tell you? So that's why you got a prickle in your foot, because you were disobedient and went past the corner! I've a mind to tell your father to leave that prickle in your foot as a punishment for disobedience. I thought I told you: not a step past the corner!"

Jack hung his head. "Come on," said his father.

"You were lucky, my boy," said Mrs Jackman, "that a cannibal swagger didn't come along and eat you, for going past the corner."

Jack's father said, "Give us your foot up here."

"If your father had any sense, he'd liven you up with that needle. Next time you want to go droving with Andy and Old Drumble, we'll have to think about you going beyond the corner, against my instructions."

Mr Jackman squeezed, and held up the needle with the thistle on the end.

"A tiny little prickle like that!" said Jack's mother. "You should be ashamed of yourself, carrying on like a baby, all because of a thistle that's so small I can hardly see it."

Jack put his foot on the floor and took a step, then a hop, and a jump. Mr Jackman gave him a grin and a nod.

"Wash your hands, and get up to the table. And don't throw the towel on the floor when you've finished with it, the pair of you. A couple of chains past the corner, indeed!"

As they were doing the dishes, after lunch, Jack looked at his mother, and saw she had her eye on him. He swallowed, remembered his father's warning, and said, "Andy told me a story."

"Oh, yes?"

"About the Southern Cross." Jack wondered if it was safe to tell his mother.

"Well, are you going to tell me the story or not?"

"He told me how to find south by the Cross. And how he used to steer his mobs of cattle and horses by it, when he was driving them up all the way from Napier, and across the pumice country, the Kaingaroa Plain, south of Rotorua. Did you know Andy used to take a shortcut across the head of the Rangitaiki River, till old Earle Vaile fenced off Broadlands Station?"

"Mr Vaile to you."

"Mr Vaile. The shortcut meant Andy used to head off across the Kaingaroa Plain from near the Rangitaiki boozer that used to be the Armed Constabulary fort during the Maori Wars, and he'd come out on the Rotorua road, getting towards the Waiotapu pub, the Taupo side of Rainbow Mountain. It saved them miles and miles, that shortcut, and he did it all by knowing how to find south by the Cross."

"We say 'hotel', not 'boozer', and I thought I told you to keep away from them?"

"I haven't been near the Rangitaiki pub, Mum. Nor the Waiotapu. Andy just told me about them. True! I don't even know where they are. Not really."

"Just as well!" His mother allowed herself a grim smile. "When we were children, your grandfather showed us how to find south by the Cross," she told Jack. "He always said he could tell the time by where those other two stars were, the ones he used to call the pointers."

"Andy said Old Drumble tells the time by the pointers, Mum, and, more often than not, he'll get it right within a couple of minutes. He told me this ancient Maori story about the Southern Cross."

"Oh, yes?"

"Thousands of years ago, there was a hero, a boy called Tai Taylor."

"Taylor? Funny name for an ancient Maori."

"It was a long time ago, and Andy said the language has probably changed a bit."

"I see," said his mother. "Taylor still doesn't sound like a very Maori name to me."

"It's in the story, how he got his name changed. You'll see it's Maori once you hear it."

"Oh, yes?" Jack's mother didn't sound very sure.

"Anyway," Jack told his mother, "there was this wild bull rampaging up and down, scaring everyone in the Waikato—"

"A bull in the Waikato! Thousands of years ago? Don't you try to bamboozle me, my boy. I know what you're up to. A bull in the Waikato? How many years ago did you say this was?"

"Andy said it was thousands of years ago," Jack told his mother. He put away a plate carefully, so he didn't chip it, and took up another. "Andy said it's one of those stories so old that it's called a — a —" He stuck on the word, tried to make its shape with his lips, but couldn't. His mother looked at him and held her mouth the same way he was holding his.

"Myth?" she asked and Jack nodded.

"How do you always know?"

"That's my secret," his mother said mysteriously. "Get on with your story."

"Andy said it's called an ancient Maori myth. Anyway, the bull was a bad-tempered Jersey. It chased everyone

174

up trees, tossed their whares in the air, and knocked down the fences. Nobody could do anything about it. People began moving to Auckland to get away from the wild bull."

"I suppose there was a city up there, Auckland, all those thousands of years ago?"

"Andy says so. In those days, this boy called Tai Taylor, lived up our end of Ward Street, in Waharoa. His house burned down a few thousand years ago, so you can't see it, but Andy says there might be a few totara piles still standing under the pig-fern on the corner of Whites' Road, if you threw a match into it and cleared it away."

"Has it occurred to you," said his mother, "that the pig-fern on the corner burns down at least twice a year, that some larrikin or other always throws a match into it when it's dry? Or that some wicked, disobedient little boy sets fire to the fern while sitting in it and smoking tobacco?" Mrs Jackman fixed Jack with her strong eye.

"I never smoke tobacco!" Jack gabbled. "Harry Jitters smoked his father's pipe once, and he was sick all over his feet. They stunk for ages. Everyone could smell them in school."

"Serves him right!" his mother declared and sniffed loudly. "I can smell tobacco on a small boy halfway down the street . . .

"If there ever were any old totara piles on that corner,

they'd have been ashes long ago," she told Jack. "You know how totara burns."

Jack wanted his mother to forget about smoking tobacco. "One day," he rattled on with his story, "the kids came out of school at three o'clock, and the bull was waiting for them outside the gate, frothing and bellowing. The girls all shrieked and ran back inside, and the boys climbed up in the chestnut trees, but Tai Taylor stood there, 'cause he was a hero and, when the bull charged, he waved his school bag in front of its nose and the bull tried to hook it with his horns.

"Tai Taylor stepped aside, and the bull followed the school bag with its eyes, so its horns missed him. It was so angry, it spun round and had another go. Tai waved his school bag, the bull followed it with its eyes, and Tai knelt so the horns went over his head.

"The third time, the bull hooked left and right and would have gored him, but Tai jumped so high the horns went under his feet. Before it could turn for another charge, Tai grabbed the bull's tail and took a turn around the trunk of the nearest chestnut tree."

Jack felt his mother's eye on him. He stopped gabbling, and blushed.

Chapter Twenty-Eight

Why the Pointers Go Around the Southern Cross, Why Mum's Mother Told Her Not to Follow Smoky Rawiri, and Why You Chip the Bark Off the Log First.

JACK FELT HIS MOTHER'S EYE on him. "Bosh! You expect me to believe that sort of taradiddle, that a bull's tail could go around one of those enormous old chestnuts?" she demanded.

"They were just little trees, all those thousands of years ago," Jack said quickly. "So the bull's tail went right round the trunk, no trouble."

"That'd be so," said his mother. Jack didn't notice the tone of her voice and plunged deeper.

"The bull was going so fast, it wound itself round the tree like a spring. When its nose was snubbed up hard against the trunk, Tai let go the tail, and the bull came off the chestnut, spinning in the other direction like a spring coming undone.

"It stood there, eyes crossed, groaning, shaking its head and horns, dizzy from all that spinning, and Tai Taylor took it by the end of its tail, swung it round and round his head, let go, and it shot bellowing up into the sky south of Waharoa.

"Ever since then, you can see the bull charging across the sky each night, and sinking out of sight towards morning. It looks as if it's hardly moving, but that's because it's so far out in the sky. Andy said so."

Jack's mother said, "He did, did he?"

"People think the Southern Cross is four stars, Mum, but it's really the bull's two eyes shining and lighting up the tips of its two horns, as it bellows and charges across the southern sky."

"And what about the two pointers? What cock-and-bull story has Andy got about them?"

"They're the two buckles on Tai's Taylor's school bag shining. When Tai swung the old bull around his head and threw him up in the sky, his horns caught the strap of Tai's school bag, and took it with him.

"That's why the pointers move around the Southern Cross, 'cause they're really the buckles shining as Tai's school bag swings round and round the bull's head like an hour hand on a clock. Andy told me how you find south by the Cross, but I can't remember how he said to tell the time by the pointers."

"And he says it's an ancient Maori myth, does he?"

Jack nodded. "He reckons, when there's a full moon and a heavy enough frost, you can hear the bull roaring away up there in the sky. With your strong ears, Mum, you'd be able to hear it."

Mrs Jackman pressed her lips together. "Go on," she said in a low voice.

"And that's how Tai got his name as a Maori hero, in memory of the day he saved all the kids at Waharoa School from the mad bull. Only, the spelling got changed over the thousands of years, so it's T-A-Y-L-O-R now instead of T-A-I-L-E-R. Andy said so."

"And where did he get that rubbish from, I'd like to know?"

"Andy said Smoky Rawiri told him the story donkey's years ago, when he was just a little boy and he ran away from home to be a drover.

"Smoky taught him lots of other ancient Maori myths," Jack told his mother. "How the waterfall out on the Kaimais was made from the tears of Roimata, the daughter of the taniwha who lives in the pool under the falls, how the Waikato River used to run through Waharoa, and how Captain Cook discovered the South Pole out in the middle of Lake Taupo.

"Smoky told Andy how Mount Te Aroha was made out of a giant ogre dancing and eating an eel on top of the Kaimais. The sun came up and turned him to stone, and the eel, too. And that's why Te Aroha sticks up above the rest of the range, and there's a tall rock like an eel along from it."

"If I close my eyes and think hard, I can just remember Smoky Rawiri," said Jack's mother. "He was a very old man when I was a little girl, wrinkled and brown from droving. He had a lovely, soft voice, and he told stories galore.

"My mother told me, 'Don't you dare listen to his stories, or you'll follow Smoky Rawiri and never come home again.'"

"Why?" Jack asked his mother.

"Because she said that Old Smoky was like the Pied Piper: only, instead of playing a pipe, he told stories, and all the children used to follow him, wanting more. And he'd lead them away under the Kaimais, and they'd never come home."

"Can you remember any of his stories?"

"I've got a house to keep clean, one that my wicked menfolk keep turning upside-down, tramping grass-cuttings through it as fast as I get it swept. Sometimes I think I might turn one of them to stone with my powerful eye."

Jack looked away from his mother's stare. "I wonder if that's what happened to Andy, when he was a little boy? Maybe he listened to Smoky Rawiri's stories, and followed him under the Kaimais, and never came home again . . .

"Mum, Andy says Smoky could tell the time by the Southern Cross, no trouble, but he'd been doing it for thousands of years. Andy said Smoky was so old, he came to New Zealand from Hawaiki in the fleet of big canoes.

Maybe he was in the one that brought the mad bull. I like those old Maori stories, Mum."

"There's plenty of wholesome Christian stories in the Bible without your needing to go listening to that rubbish. Peg that tea towel on the clothes-line. And don't you dare go mentioning to Mrs Dainty that the Southern Cross is really a mad bull charging down the sky. She's still getting over that one of Mr Lewis's getting through her fence.

"By the way——" his mother skewered him with her eye, "——what's this that Mrs Dainty told me about you growling and pretending to be a pig, a couple of weeks ago?"

"Not a pig, Mum! I was being a holding dog, grappling with a boar pig."

"Well, just grapple with that tea towel, and you can imagine you're pegging out the stars in the sky, but don't go telling Mrs Dainty I said so."

"Mum?" asked Jack, in a singsong voice. "Mu-um?"

"What do you want now?" His mother wiped the bench, wrung out the dishcloth, and tossed it to him to peg out as well.

"Mum, if you can smell tobacco on me from thirty feet away, does that mean you've got a strong nose like your strong ears and your strong eye?"

"John Jackman, if you're not pegging out that tea towel and dishcloth by the time I've counted to three, you'll feel the back of my strong hand. One! Two!—" But Jack was gone.

He kept a watch for the next few days, but Andy didn't come driving stock through Waharoa and, the following Saturday, Mr Murdoch gave Jack and his father a lift out to Mr Barker's farm on the Wardville road.

They took a billy, some tea leaves in an Edmonds Baking Powder tin, a couple of tin mugs, a bottle of milk, a jam jar filled with sugar, a newspaper-wrapped packet of sandwiches, and a couple of apples. They also took a sack with a couple of other sacks pushed into the bottom, some wedges, an axe, a maul, a length of stick polished by use, an oily rag, a round sharpening stone, a triangular file, and the big cross-cut saw. They put everything on the back of the lorry, and heaved up the bike as well.

As they drove past Griffiths's corner, Jack looked at the spabs' nest in the big poplar and wondered if swaggers climbed trees and ate birds' eggs. They drove past the turn-off, and he stared at the yellow A.A. sign that said: "Te Aroha". At Mr Barker's letter-box, they unloaded their gear. Mr Jackman put a pikau with the tucker on his back, balanced the heavy sack and the cross-cut on the bike and pushed it, and Jack carried the billy and the bottle of milk.

Up the drive, they left the bike by a gate, and carried everything across to a shelter-belt where wind rolling back off the Kaimais had blown over two pines and a dead bluegum.

"We'll saw through the pine first, and get it split — before it gets too tough. Then we'll get on to the gum; it'll burn okay this winter. The pine'll be best kept to dry for the winter after."

Jack tried to think of the winter after the next winter, and found he couldn't manage it. "Will I be old by then?" he asked.

"About a year and a bit older, that's all. Grab that stick out of the sack and poke it through the other end of the cross-cut, and you can give me a hand."

Mr Jackman started chipping off the thick bark around the pine log. "It can clog up the teeth on the saw," he said.

Chapter Twenty-Nine

Splitting With the Grain, What the Oily Rag Was For, and the Story of the Floating Island That Drifts Up and Down the Waihou River.

MR JACKMAN STOOD ONE SIDE of the log, Jack the other, the cross-cut balanced on its teeth in the nick taken out with the axe.

"Let it run back and forwards," his father told Jack a few minutes later, "so the saw does the cutting itself. If there's a secret to using a cross-cut, that's it."

Letting the saw cut by itself was a hard lesson. They made a couple of cuts through the pine, then Jack was happy to take his handle out of the end of the cross-cut and let his father saw by himself, while he filled the billy at a trough.

Jack took care not to get any water out of the trough into the billy, because you never knew what bugs there might be in that stuff. There was just room to get the billy under the dribble of water coming from the pipe at the ball cock. As he walked back across the paddock, the wire handle hurt him, and he looked and saw a raised blister on the palm of that hand, and one on the other.

He pushed one, then the other, and they looked full of whitish watery stuff.

He collected a few pine cones, and built a tiny stack of splinters from dry sticks he'd found under the shelter-belt. His father tossed him his tin of wax matches, and Jack scratched one on the bottom, got the splinters going, and fed twigs into the flames till they caught fire, and he could put on the cones. He couldn't get a stick deep enough in the ground, so his father belted one in with the back of his axe, and Jack hung the billy off a notch.

Mr Barker came across for a yarn, and had a mug of tea with them. His cattle dog sat and watched from a distance. Although Jack looked, it didn't look back at him.

"You can stack the pine along the fence; it'll dry out good-oh," Mr Barker said. "There's always a draught under a shelter-belt. How are your hands?" he asked Jack.

Jack showed him. "They say there's only one thing to fix blisters," Mr Barker said. "Keep sawing so they burst and form scabs. Once your hands are hard enough, you don't get any more."

"Doesn't it hurt?"

"You bet! Some men piss on their hands, saying it stops the blisters. Some reckon that meths will harden your hands, too, but there's always the danger you'll start drinking it." Mr Barker laughed and strode away, his dog slipping behind him.

"I'll finish this cut and do some splitting. How about filling a sack with cones? That won't hurt your hands, and then you could have a look in the drain. You might spot an eel."

The dry pine cones were bigger and lighter, because their wooden petals were open, so the sack filled quickly. The green cones were closed tight, and heavy. When he twisted one, to get it off the branch, it tore a blister open. Watery fluid gushed, and Jack looked at the pink skin inside the blister and didn't like it. Blowing on it made it sore, so he went over to the drain. It had been cleaned, the weeds thrown on the banks, and he couldn't see any eels. A couple of pukekos stalked between clumps of reeds, the other side of the drain, flicking their white patches.

When the pooks vanished, Jack wandered back, listening to the thump! thump! of the maul, and boiled the billy for lunch.

They'd eaten their sandwiches, and his father was doing some more splitting, when Jack looked across the paddock to the road and saw somebody trotting towards the Kaimais. It was Andy on Nosy, with Old Drumble leading, Young Nugget and Old Nell behind. Jack climbed on a stump and waved and yelled till they went out of sight behind a hedge, but they hadn't looked his way.

"You might not be seeing so much of Andy in future," said his father. "Put those lengths on the stack. You'll need a good bath tonight, to get all the pine gum off your elbows and knees, and I don't know what your mother's going to say about getting it all over your clobber."

"Mum said it didn't matter, 'cause these are old. 'Just don't you dare go getting it in your hair,' she said, 'or I'll have to snip it off with the scissors,' and she said did I want to look piebald for when school starts."

His father grinned. "I could shave your head all over, with my cut-throat razor."

"Harry Jitters would bark and say I looked like a sheep. I should never have told him about how huntaways bark. And Minnie Mitchell wouldn't talk to me, if I was bald.

"Dad, do you think Mum will let me go droving with Andy next holidays?" Jack watched his father bring down the axe exactly, so the length of pine sprang into clean billets. He sniffed the sharp smell of the fresh-faced wood and said, "I wish I could chop where I mean to."

"It's like using a bat — and keeping your eye on the ball: you keep your eye on the spot you want to hit, Jack, and the axe does the rest." Whack! Another piece leapt off. "Look for the grain, and split with it. See! And always split down the middle of a knot, with its grain — never across it." Whack!

"I don't know about droving with Andy, next holidays,"

said Mr Jackman. "That's what I meant about not seeing so much of him in future.

"Andy's getting a bit long in the tooth; he's been at it a few years now, you know."

"What's he going to do?"

"Everyone's got to give up, sooner or later, and Andy's had a pretty good innings. He picked up the job from Smoky Rawiri, and he's been dead half a lifetime. Andy had already been droving for years, when your mother was just a girl. It's not the easiest of lives, outside in all weather, handling half-wild steers, nasty-tempered Jersey bulls, and sheep that don't know which way they want to go."

"They do when Old Drumble leads them."

"True!" His father was putting his wedges in the sack and stowing them under a log. He wiped the saw — especially the teeth — with the oily rag. "So it doesn't rust," he said. "A rusty saw makes the job harder." He rolled the triangular file in the rag and stowed it away with the cross-cut and the axe.

They finished stacking the split firewood, emptied the billy on the ashes, and put it away upside-down in a dry spot under a stump, with the mugs, the tin of tea leaves and the sugar jar.

"Drink what's left of the milk, and put the bottle in the pikau." His father was putting away a handful of twigs and some cones for lighting the fire next time, stuffing with them the newspaper that had wrapped their sandwiches.

"We don't want to leave a mess, not when Mr Barker's doing us a good turn. Your behind's going to be sore, sitting on the bar all the way into Waharoa."

"I don't mind, Dad. It's good fun."

Down the drive, Jack looked at some pellets of sheep shit and said, "I told Harry Jitters they were Smarter Pills, and he ate a handful and said he wasn't any smarter, and I told him, 'Now you're a-gettin' smarter!'"

Mr Jackman snorted. "Where did you hear that?"

"You said it to Mr Murdoch," said Jack, "and you both laughed, so I thought I'd try it on Harry."

"You'll get me into trouble yet," chuckled his father. "Look out! What are you up to?" They were turning out on to the road.

"I was trying to see if I could spot Andy and Old Drumble."

"They were going out to pick up some steers off Brooks's place, out under the Kaimais," his father told him. "By now they should be on their way back, heading for the Gordon bridge. Andy's driving the steers over to the works at Horotiu."

"He used to take steers from up the Tapu Valley, and from down Opotiki, and Poverty Bay, and graze them along the side of the road, all the way up to the Auckland sales," Jack said. "He told me stories about them."

"I'll bet he did . . . "

"He told me about where the old drovers go to die."

"I haven't heard that one." They were passing the Wardville school, and Mick O'Halloran's whare where two herring-gutted dogs leapt and barked on their chains.

"Andy says there's a floating island that was born out in the Hauraki Gulf or the Firth of Thames, and it drifts up and down the Waihou River, up past Okauia Springs as far as the falls at Okoroire, and then down again."

"Go on," said his father.

Chapter Thirty

Rump Steak and the Knife and Steel Dance, Some Day When We're Rich, and Why Jack's Mother Asked if Her Ears Were Deceiving Her.

"SOMETIMES," SAID JACK, "the floating island's just a patch of flax and raupo, sometimes it's a huge island with lots of bush and grassy clearings, mountains, hills, beaches, its own rivers and creeks, even a couple of lakes. Andy says it even has its own weather.

"Sometimes it comes aground in the Waihou out at the Gordon, and Smoky Rawiri used to use it as a bridge to drive steers and sheep across, but mostly they had to put them across at the ford. That was when Andy was a little boy and ran away from home to become a drover.

"Once, they put a mob of steers on to the island, and it drifted off downstream before they could get the dogs and horses on board. It didn't stop till it had floated out past Thames, across the Firth, up past Waiheke and Brown's Island, and into Auckland, where it came aground in Mechanics Bay, and they ran the steers ashore, and drove them out down the Great South Road, for the sales."

"That must have been handy," said Mr Jackman.

"Yes, but Smoky and Andy had to do the barking and chase the steers themselves, then walk all the way back over the Bombay Hills and across the Hauraki Plain up to the Gordon, to collect their dogs and horses. Andy said Old Drumble and Nosy thought it was a great joke."

Jack felt his father laughing to himself, and he thought he liked being doubled on the bike, his father's arms around him. He looked at the top of the front tyre, how it kept coming out from under the mudguard and disappearing, yet it never stopped.

"They got the top price at the sales," he said, "because the steers had eaten everything green on the island and put on a fair bit of weight. They even stripped the branches of the pussy willows. And, not having done much walking, they were in prime condition."

"Crikey!" said his father.

"Dad, am I in prime condition?"

"I reckon," said Mr Jackman, "if I was to double you all the way up to the Auckland sales and sell you there, you'd bring the top price. You weigh enough, so you must be in prime condition." He puffed noisily and pedalled as if it was hard going.

"Do you want me to ride, and give you a dub?"

"I don't know if your legs are long enough to reach the pedals yet. What else did Andy tell you about the old drovers' cemetery?"

"The floating island, it's still there, drifting up and

down the Waihou, and round the Hauraki Gulf, only you've got to believe in it to be able to see it. Andy said it's where Smoky Rawiri went after he died, and all the other old drovers. And their horses and dogs.

"I don't think Mum could see the floating island, Dad, because she wouldn't believe in it, would she?"

"Maybe not."

"Andy said all the old drovers and their old horses and dogs never have to do any droving again. They spend their days fishing and swimming, pig hunting and collecting driftwood, and each night they light a big campfire, and sit around grilling the best cuts of rump steak on sticks in front of the embers, singing, drinking whisky, and telling yarns. And one night each year, they do the knife and steel dance."

"The knife and steel dance?"

"You have to dance around the fire, sharpening your skinning knife on the steel with your eyes closed and not cutting yourself, and you jump backwards and forwards through the flames, balancing the tip of your skinning knife on your nose. Andy said it's a very old drover's dance. The best dancer and storyteller wins a barrel of whisky."

"What if it's a horse or a dog? The winner I mean."

"They get the barrel of whisky, just like anyone else. Dogs and horses love whisky, Andy said. Remember Old Drumble's kennel?"

"I haven't forgotten Old Drumble's kennel; nor has your mother. I don't think she'll ever look on Old Drumble in quite the same way. You're probably better keeping it to yourself: the floating island, and the barrel of whisky for a prize. There are some things it's best not to tell Mum."

"But that wouldn't be honest, would it, Dad?"

His father pedalled a couple of chains before he replied. "It's pretty tricky I know but, as you get older, you learn when to say things, and when not to. Tell Mum your stories, by all means, but she doesn't want to know about Old Drumble's boozing, not really. And I'd be a bit chary about the knife and steel dance, too. I don't think she'd like that."

They biked past the Te Aroha turn-off, Jack staring at the yellow A.A. signpost. "I've never been to Te Aroha," he sighed.

"Some day when we've paid off the mortgage on the house, we'll buy a car and drive over to Te Aroha, Mum and me in the front, and you in the dicky seat, and we'll stop in the middle of the bridge, and see if we can spot Andy's floating island in the Waihou."

"Andy said old Henry Rawiri called the floating island a motu tapu," Jack told his father.

"A sacred island," said Mr Jackman. "There's a big island in the Gulf by that name: Motutapu. Only Aucklanders call it Motor-tap."

194

Jack laughed. "Motor-tap!" he said. "Dad, when I grow up, will I be able to drive cattle from down past Opotiki all the way up to Auckland for the sales?"

"I don't know how long they'll keep up those big drives," Mr Jackman told Jack, "fattening them on the long acre. Somebody said one day they're going to build lorries big enough just for carrying stock. And more and more of them go by train these days. The drover's life will come to an end."

"Is Andy going to die?"

"I just mean things are changing," said Jack's father. "There'll always be the local drives, so long as there's the weekly sales at Matamata and Morrinsville, and sharemilkers shifting their herds from farm to farm on Gypsy Day. But the big drives, nobody can tell how long they'll last. When I was a boy, the old drovers used to talk of driving mobs from one end of the North Island to the other, taking up land. And the same down south."

Jack tried to think of the roads without Andy driving sheep and cattle along them, without Old Drumble trotting ahead, tail waving like a black and white flag. "If there isn't going to be any droving, then Old Drumble can become a pisshead," he said. "It won't matter, so long as he's not on the road. Andy told me."

"You might say that to me," said his father, "but I'd shy off saying it to your mother; I certainly wouldn't go saying 'pisshead' in her hearing. Andy and Old

Drumble wouldn't want you getting into trouble on their account."

"I suppose not," Jack agreed.

He shifted his behind on the bar, and remembered not to grab at the handlebars. "Are we coming out to cut firewood next weekend?"

"I hope to," said his father. "Maybe we can get a lift both ways with Bob Murdoch, then Harry could come along, too. He'd be company for you."

"I wouldn't mind that," said Jack. "It'd be good if we could have Andy and Old Drumble for company, too, and Mum, of course. She's company, even if she does strong-eye me sometimes and makes me tell her all Andy's stories about Old Drumble and Nosy.

"I don't suppose Minnie Mitchell would want to come cutting firewood," Jack said. "Girls aren't interested in learning how to use a cross-cut and split with the grain, things like that."

"It's not the sort of thing girls do."

"Mum can. She reckons it's just as well she knows how to use an axe," Jack told his father. "When I forget to chop the kindling, or break up a butter box for her to burn under the copper, she says it's quicker to do it herself than wait for me to remember. That's when she says, 'If a job's worth doing, it's worth doing well.'"

"I've heard her say that on occasion."

They came round the Wardville turn-off on to the

main road, and the dairy factory was in sight. Jack looked for the top of the brick chimney sticking above the roofs at the far end.

"And she says, 'If I waited for you and your father to keep me in kindling wood, I'd still be waiting in another hundred years.'"

"Your mother's a redoubtable woman, but don't go telling her I said that." Mr Jackman grunted and shoved on the pedals. "I didn't know there was a hill here." They came up the slight rise past Caseys' place, where Jack looked at the big trees.

"I like walnuts," he said.

"It'll be months before they're ripe. Almost home now."

Around the church corner, past Harry's and Minnie's, past the pig-fern and the bamboo, up the top end of Ward Street, and in the gate.

"Mum!" Jack yelled. "We're home! Did you know Old Drumble's going to give up droving and become a pisshead?"

"Are my ears deceiving me?" said his mother.

Chapter Thirty-One

Something I Can Eat in My Hand,
Trouble With Willows, and
Never the Same Again.

"I TOLD YOU TO SHUT UP about that," Jack's father muttered, then gabbled: "Hello, dear! We got a good lot of firewood sawn and split, and the boy was a great help. By Jove, he's getting to be a weight, doubling him on the bike."

"My behind's sore." Jack felt for his father's foot, slid off the bar, and rubbed himself.

"It's going to be a sight sorer, if I hear you using language like that, my boy — oh, that'll be the telephone! Answer it for me. Why it always chooses to ring, just when I'm about to put tea on the table . . . "

Jack pushed the stool to the wall, stood on it so he could reach to speak into the mouthpiece, and held the receiver on its cord to his ear.

"Nine K!"

"Is your dad there?"

"Dad, it's for you."

"Are you there? Oh, it's you, Bob . . . Why, what's up?"

Mrs Jackman stopped whisking the mashed potatoes around with a fork and turned and stared at Jack's father.

"What do you mean 'gone'?" Mr Jackman said into the telephone and listened. "I'll be ready by the time you get here. See you." He hung up the earpiece and turned the little handle to ring off.

"What's happened?" asked Mrs Jackman.

Jack felt uneasy at the way his mother was standing, at the way she and his father were looking at each other. Had he done something wrong?

"Old Andy. They found his horse out at the Gordon, on the shingle downstream of the bridge."

"Nosy," said Jack.

"No sign of him. Steers up and down the river-bed and all over the road. We're going to give a hand to search the river. The trouble is all those willows."

"You get some food inside you before you go."

"Give me something I can eat in my hand." Mr Jackman was already chewing a chop as he talked, shoving his boots back on, helping himself to a mouthful of mashed potato, another chop, doing up his laces. Mrs Jackman was pouring boiling water from the kettle on the stove into the teapot and saying, "Jack, pop out and ask Mr Murdoch to come in and have a cup of tea, while your father has a bite to eat.

"You can't go back all the way out there, searching

into the night, with nothing in your stomach. And you see you take care among those willows. Treacherous things. I don't know why the County Council doesn't get rid of them, growing their roots into the river, causing floods.

"It's quite all right, Jack, you sit down and get on with your tea. Hello, Mr Murdoch. Here's a sad thing, by the sound of it."

Again, it was something not just in their voices, but in the silences between them, their glances.

"What's wrong?" Jack's own voice was uncertain.

"Nothing's wrong. Well, nothing that we know of yet. You just get on with your tea." His mother pushed him down into his chair. "Take care now. It'll be dark before you know where you are," and she was standing at the door, bunching her apron in her left hand, holding the teapot in her right, watching his father and Mr Murdoch go out to the lorry, listening to it drive away towards the bottom end of Ward Street.

"What's happened to Andy, Mum?"

"Far too old to be droving still, a man of his years!"

"Is he all right?"

"Nobody knows anything yet. It could all be a false alarm. We'll find out soon enough."

Jack would have liked to chew his chop in his hand, too, but he cut around the meat on the inside of the bone, cut a small slice off that, and jabbed his fork into it. "What about Old Drumble?" he asked.

"Oh, the dog'll look after himself. A sight better than a man in the river."

"Did Andy fall in the river?"

"I told you we don't know. It looks as if he might have come off his horse. Now, you just get on and eat up your tea."

"We saw Andy and Old Drumble, this morning, Mum. They were heading out to pick up a mob of steers off Brooks's place, out under the Kaimais."

"Did you speak to them?"

"They were too far away to hear, but I climbed on a stump and waved till they went out of sight."

"I'm sure he'll be all right. Your father'll tell us everything when he gets home. Typical man. I wish he'd had time to eat a proper meal, and look — he didn't even take a mouthful out of his cup of tea."

"What's the trouble with willows, Mum?"

"Some people say they hold the banks together, but a lot of others say they cause floods. I've never liked them. Untidy things, the way they take over . . .

"Come on now, eat up your tea while it's hot. There's another chop, if you've got room for it. And plenty of potato. And I made you a golden syrup pudding because that's your favourite. And your father's. Although he does like a suet pudding, what he will call a plum duff. I'll hot it up for him, when he comes home. And I'll put his plate into the oven, though I'm afraid it'll be dried up by the time he gets back."

Jack had stopped chewing and was staring at his mother, as she plumped into his father's chair, her fingers pleating her apron, smiling at him, tears spilling and running down her cheeks.

"There's no need to worry. Everything's going to be all right. Oh, those blessed rivers! I've never trusted them. And the horses. You never know when they're going to shy at a bird flying up, or a leaf blowing across the road."

"Old Drumble's there," said Jack. "He'll look after Andy. He'll drag him out on the floating island."

"The floating island! What on earth is the boy talking about now?" His mother's voice had changed because the telephone had rung again, and she was answering it.

"No, not a thing. Yes, they were just coming in the door, and the telephone rang, and it was Mr Murdoch, and the next thing he was here; that'd be when you saw him driving past. And my hubby rushed out the door, gulping at something in his hand as he went—

"Goodness only knows. Look, I'm just giving the boy his tea, but I'll ring you the moment I hear anything. Yes. Yes. Goodbye. Goodbye.

"Trust her. Not a movement around the village, but she's awake to it. I should have known she'd be listening in, on the party line." His mother was talking to herself, but Jack

202

knew by her voice whom it had been on the telephone.

"Now, what's all this nonsense about a floating island?"

Jack stared back at his mother and remembered his father's warning. "It's just a story Andy told me, about a floating island in the Waihou River."

"Yes, well he's got stories enough to fill a book, if anyone had the energy to write them down, let alone the time to read them. Would you like some cream with your pudding? There's plenty. Oh, there it goes ringing again. Here, help yourself."

Much later, Jack woke, and it was dark. There were voices in the kitchen, light shining under the door. He heard his father's voice, and his mother. And that was Mr Murdoch. But that was somebody else, another man. More noises, feet tramping. A lorry door slammed, then a second time, harder, so he knew it was Mr Murdoch's. His bedroom door opened, and his mother appeared against the light.

"Are you asleep?"

He closed his eyes, lay still, and said nothing. His mother paused. "Everything'll be all right," she said, but her voice was funny, and he knew as she stooped and kissed him that things were not all right, that they were never going to be the same again. Then the light went out, the door closed, and he must have slept.

Chapter Thirty-Two

Getting a Dub Home.

"WE COULD PLAY DROVERS," said Harry Jitters to Jack Jackman one afternoon after school. They were sitting with their backs to the mouth of the tunnel into the pig-fern at the corner of Whites' Road and Ward Street.

The week before, Mr Strap had opened the school door and rung the bell at nine o'clock, and the long holidays were over. The only time for play now was after hometime at three o'clock.

"We could play drovers," Harry said again.

"Who wants to do that? Walking along behind smelly sheep all day." Neither of them had heard Minnie Mitchell coming back from the shops. She stood, looking down at them.

"Playing drovers!" said Minnie, and Jack felt his mouth water, as she tore a flakey bit from the end of the loaf in her basket and licked it off her fingers with a pink tongue like a cat's. "Some day they're going to take the stock route around behind Waharoa, so they don't come along the residential end of Ward Street."

"I get a hiding if I eat the kissing bread," said Harry.

"I'm allowed." Minnie tore off a bit more, and Jack

swallowed. "Anyway," she said to him, "I don't know any old drovers; you're the one who knew him."

"Knew who?"

"That old drover."

"I don't know any old drover!"

"You do so, Jack Jackman. You knew the one who got drowned with his dog, out in the river at the Gordon."

"I know where old drovers and their dogs go when they die," said Jack.

"They buried him down the cemetery," said Harry. "My father went to the funeral, and he said your dad helped carry the coffin, and your mother was there, and she was crying."

"She was not," said Jack.

"She was so."

"She was not!"

"You weren't allowed to go to the funeral, so how would you know, Jack Jackman?" said Minnie.

Harry nodded. "My father said, after they filled in the grave, they'd heap up the dirt this high, and cover it with the wreaths of flowers. I wonder why they heap up the dirt so high, on top of a grave?"

"That's because there wasn't anything inside Andy's coffin," said Jack. "It was empty, so when the coffin collapses, the dirt'll settle down." He sounded quite certain. "That wasn't Andy and Old Drumble, in the coffin; not really."

"Aw! Where are they then?"

"On the floating island where old drovers and their dogs go when they die. And their horses. They don't have to drive sheep and cattle any more; they just hunt pigs all day, and all night they sit round the campfire, singing and drinking and telling yarns.

"And when the drovers get half-cut, they do the knife and steel dance, and they jump through the flames with the tips of their skinning knives balanced on their noses. Andy told me."

"You made that up!"

"And because they're pissed, the flames don't burn them."

"Oooh! Jack Jackman, you swore."

"And the dog that tells the best bullshit story gets a barrel of whisky, and he drinks it empty and sleeps in it for a kennel."

"I'm telling my mother on you, Jack Jackman."

As Minnie ran, crying and waving her basket, towards the bottom end of Ward Street, Harry asked, "What's the knife and steel dance?" but Jack had disappeared. Harry thought he might as well go home, too, just in case.

Deep in the fern, Jack sat in his secret possie. He didn't think Minnie's mother would understand about the floating island, and Old Drumble and his barrel of whisky. Mrs Dainty hadn't understood either, when he'd tried to tell her, and then she'd spun round and caught him saying, "Unga-Yunga!" and pulling a face after her.

He'd got into trouble for that, yet he'd only been trying to tell her that Andy and Old Drumble were all right.

His father understood and, after he told her, his mother understood, too. She said it was rather a lovely story, when you come to think of it. But she still said there was no need to go repeating that bit about the dog and the barrel of whisky. Certainly not to Mrs Dainty.

"I thought you'd have more sense by now, John Jackman," his mother told him.

Jack stuck his head out of the pig-fern, and looked towards the bottom end of Ward Street. His father said you had to take people as you found them, but he wasn't sure what that meant; it didn't help much, not when they were like Mrs Dainty.

He watched Harry running towards his gate and gave a bark, not as good as Old Drumble's bark, of course, but still not bad, a noisy huntaway bark, just to give Harry a hurry-up. He barked again and knelt out of sight in the fern in case.

When he went home, he'd tell Mum what he'd said to Minnie and Harry about Old Drumble and the knife and steel dance, and she'd say, "I thought I told you not to repeat that word."

The factory whistle blew for five o'clock. Jack looked through the pig-fern towards the bottom end of Ward

Street, for his father's bike. He'd get a double home, and Dad would listen to how he'd told the story of the floating island to Minnie and Harry, and he'd understand. He'd be okay there, sitting on the bar with his father's arms around him, stopping him from falling off. He'd hold his feet well out, so they wouldn't get caught in the spokes.

Jack crawled out and sat and waited at the end of the tunnel.

Glossary

alky An alcoholic; somebody who can't stop drinking.

Armed Constabulary Armed and uniformed men who kept civil order, like police, 1846–1886, and fought like soldiers in the Land Wars. In 1886, the Armed Constabulary was split into the New Zealand Police Force and the Army.

ball cock The floating ball that controls the water level in a trough.

bamboozle To fool somebody.

basic slag A fertiliser farmers used to help grass grow.

batten A light length of wood used between posts to hold fence wires apart.

beak Slang for a magistrate or judge.

beaut Excellent, very good.

belting the hops along Drinking a lot of alcohol.

bicycle clips Men wore clips on their trouser cuffs to stop them getting caught in the chain. Women's bikes had a netting cover over the back wheel to protect their long dresses.

biddy Woman; often meant critically.

bight The bend or loop in the end of a pair of reins, or in a rope.

Bill Masseys Heavy boots got this name from the army boots issued to soldiers during the Great War, when the prime minister was William Massey.

birdcage The small paddock where horses are paraded before a race.

Blarney Stone If you kiss the Blarney Stone in Ireland, you can talk people into believing anything. And if you believe that sort of nonsense, you'll believe anything.

blaspheme To insult religion.

Blondin A man who was famous for walking the tightrope across high places.

bob A shilling in the old money. Twelve pennies made a shilling, two shillings made a florin, and twenty shillings made a pound.

bookie Somebody who took illegal bets on the races. If the horse won, the bookie paid out; if it lost, the bookie kept the money. If the police caught him, the bookie went to prison.

border collie A breed of sheep dog, often strong-eyed, usually black and white, and used for heading sheep.

bosh Nonsense.

breaking in Clearing land for a farm.

bully, a bit of bully A dog with a bit of bull terrier in him.

bush-burn seed Cheap grass seed sown in the ashes after the bush and scrub was burnt off.

butcher's hook To go crook. (Rhyming slang.)

carrier A man who owned a lorry for carrying cans of milk and cream to the dairy factory, and spent the rest of the day taking loads from the railway station out to the farms, and goods to the shops.

cattle beast A cow or steer; sometimes used for wild cattle. You can't talk of two cattle, but you can say "Two or three cattle beasts."

chain An old measurement of twenty-two yards, about twenty metres.

chary Careful, wary.

chiacking Teasing.

chivvy To chase.

chook A hen — or what we now call a chicken.

chops Jaws.

clearfell To clear land by chopping down the trees and scrub.

clobber Clothes.

clucky A hen which clucks a lot, showing she's ready to hatch eggs and bring up the chickens.

cock-and-bull story A made-up story, a lie.

cocky A farmer.

collywobbles Stomach pains, the trots or diarrhoea.

comfrey A plant that people thought was healing; now thought to be dangerous.

coot An odd, unreasonable person.

copper Maori A hangi or umu — an underground oven.

corker Good.

cough up Pay up.

cracking, to get cracking To get going.

Crimson Glory A scented red rose.

crook Sick.

cut down Model A An old Ford car with the body cut down to make a light truck.

dags Wool clotted with dung.

dicky seat A folding seat on the back of old cars — where the boot is today. Riding outside in the dicky seat was fun!

dog-tucker To kill something for dog food.

double, dub A ride on the bar of a bicycle.

down, to have a down on something To dislike it.

down to it Sorry for himself. Out of luck.

drain A ditch.

dry area Some districts in New Zealand didn't have pubs, and they were called dry.

dry fly A trout hook made to look like a floating fly — and cast upstream.

dub A double on a bike.

dunny Slang for lavatory, what's now called the toilet.

E. Earle Vaile An early farmer on the pumice lands of the volcanic plateau. He wrote an interesting book, *Pioneering the Pumice*.

elbow grease, put some elbow grease into it Work harder!

eye dog A strong-eye dog.

F.A.C. Farmers Auctioneering Company, a cooperative company (like the Farmers' Trading Company) that ran general stores for farmers.

fag A cigarette.

Fair Isle A Shetland Islands knitting pattern for jerseys.

fib A small lie.

flatties Flounder, flatfish.

ford A shallow place where you can cross a river.

Free Lance An old New Zealand magazine.

furlong An old measurement for ten chains or about two hundred metres.

gallows A wooden frame used to hang people.

galore Lots.

gaolbird Somebody in prison.

gelding A castrated male horse.

gob Mouth.

Golden Delicious A sweet gold-green apple.

goorie Mongrel. An Anglicised (turned into English) form of the Maori word **kuri** — which means a dog.

Granny Smith A green-skinned apple.

Great War The First World War, 1914–1918.

grid A bicycle.

gutsful A bellyful, too much.

Gypsy Day 1 June, the day that sharemilkers who were shifting farms used to move their herds, their families, and gear.

half-cut Half-drunk.

hammer, **on my hammer** Pestering and bothering me.

handle A glass beer mug with a handle.

handy dog One that will work both as a huntaway and a heading dog. An all-rounder.

hangied Cooked underground in a hangi.

hard stuff Strong liquor, especially whisky.

haver To muck around, not knowing what to do, dithering.

having him on Teasing him.

hawser Heavy rope.

head To run ahead and turn back sheep or cattle. So, we say a **header**, or a **heading dog**. Heading dogs' barks are quiet; they don't bark much.

herring-gutted Skinny.

hinaki An eel trap; also used for prison.

hit the turps Heavy drinking of alcohol. Here it means that Tuppenny Bill turned to getting drunk every day.

hitting the bottle Drinking a lot of alcohol.

holder A dog that will stop and hold a wild pig.

honk To smell badly.

hoofed it Walked.

horse paddock Country schools often had a horse paddock, because many children rode to school. The same paddock was used for playing footy.

hullabaloo Noise.

huntaway A noisy dog for driving sheep forward. A good huntaway will bark when told.

hurry-up An encouragement to hurry.

inch An old measurement of about two and a half centimetres.

Institute The New Zealand Countrywomen's Institute. Meetings were usually on a Wednesday afternoon, in country districts, while the farmers were at the weekly stock sales.

Jeez! A slang form of Jesus as an exclamation. Gee! might be a shorter form of the same word.

Jersey A common breed of cow in New Zealand.

jumping the broomstick A sham wedding in which the partners sometimes jump over a broomstick and say they are married.

kindling Fine-split wood for lighting a fire.

kissing-bread The tasty, flakey bread where a double loaf is broken into two.

knife and steel dance A dangerous dance that used to be performed by deer cullers and high country musterers.

komaty Dead. Anglicised (turned into English) from the Maori **ka mate**.

larrikins Yahoos, hoodlums.

lavatory, lavvy, lav Toilet.

lawsoniana A common hedge tree on farms.

leading dog A dog that will take the lead in front of a mob of sheep, showing them the way, and stopping them from breaking and running wild.

leery Cunning, suspicious.

Lent A period when Christians remember Jesus going without food in the wilderness — by going without something themselves.

lit out Took off, ran away.

long acre The grass along the side of a road.

long in the tooth Old.

loony bin A mental hospital. Loony — from lunatic.

magistrate What we used to call a judge in a lower court in New Zealand.

Maori Wars What we now call the Land Wars.

maul A heavy wooden-headed hammer for driving wedges.

meths Methylated spirits. Drinking it can make you blind and kill you.

moe Sleep (Maori).

mooch To wander or stroll.

mosey A look around.

nag Horse.

nick Run or take a shortcut.

nicker A pound in the old money.

nineteen to the dozen Talking very fast without stopping.

not on your Nelly Rhyming slang: Not on your Nelly Duff = puff = life. So it means "Not on your life!" or "Not likely!"

nut case A mad person.

on the swag Carrying a swag, that is being a swagger — on the road.

out the monk Asleep, drunk, or unconscious.

over the moon Excited.

pagan Non-Christian.

Phar Lap A famous racehorse which was born in New Zealand, won lots of races including the Melbourne Cup in Australia, and died — perhaps of poison — in the U.S.A. You can see his stuffed hide in the Melbourne museum, or his skeleton in Wellington museum.

perked up Cheered up.

pie funnel A china support for a piecrust during cooking. It usually has a hole for letting out steam.

Pied Piper If you don't know it, ask your teacher to read you "The Pied Piper of Hamelin", a poem by Robert Browning.

pikau A big sack sewn up at both ends, split open across the middle of one side, and thrown over a horse's back to make a large bag either side. Also the usual name for a sugarbag used as a backpack. **Pikau** is a Maori word meaning to carry on the back, to piggyback somebody.

piss Alcohol, usually beer.

pisshead A drunkard.

plastered Drunk.

Plymouth An American car.

Plymouth Brethren A Christian religious movement.

point the finger To accuse somebody.

pointers The two bright stars, Alpha and Beta Centauri, which seem to point to the Southern Cross, and to move around it.

pooks Pukekos.

poorman's orange Grapefruit.

possie A safe place of your own, a favourite spot, sometimes a hiding place.

poultice Something soft and hot that is bandaged on to a wound or sore to relieve pain and stop infection. People said a hot poultice would "draw" a boil.

province A region of New Zealand, for example, the Waikato Province.

pub-crawl Having a drink in every pub in a street or town.

puku Belly.

punt A flat-bottomed, shallow, square-ended boat, usually poled rather than rowed.

push A bunch or gang of people.

quack Doctor.

quid One pound in old money.

rampage To behave violently, out of control.

raupo A tall New Zealand swamp plant, a bulrush.

Rawleighs Man A travelling salesman for the Rawleighs Company, selling many household and medical items to people who couldn't get to town.

rheumatism What we now call arthritis.

Rhode Island Red A breed of hen.

ringbark To chop a ring of bark from around a tree, killing it.

rubbing strake A length of timber to protect the side of a boat from rubbing against a wharf.

run-in Trouble, an argument.

saddle-tweed A thick woollen material used for men's trousers. They were warm and hard-wearing.

saleyards Wooden-fenced yards where stock are sold.

sand-shoes Cheap canvas shoes like sneakers, worn by many people without jobs during the 1920s and 1930s.

scow Flat-bottomed sailing ship common on the New Zealand coast up to about the Second World War.

School Journal A reader or magazine in New Zealand schools.

schooner A very tall beer glass that holds a lot.

setting A number of eggs set under a clucky hen for hatching.

shambles A mess.

shelter-belt A row of trees for breaking the wind.

shy off Avoid doing something.

skedaddled Ran off.

skewer To pierce something; to look sharply at somebody.

skinful Enough to make somebody drunk.

skittle Knock over.

skulduggery Dishonest trick.

sleepers Heavy hardwood beams that railway lines used to be laid upon. Nowadays, they're often concrete.

Soldiers' Settlement A district of farms settled by returned soldiers after the Great War.

sool To set a dog on to somebody.

spab Sparrow.

spalpeen A boy.

sprag A sharp piece of wire.

Stan Goosman The owner of a large fleet of trucks. He became a member of parliament, Minister of Railways and Public Works, and was knighted.

steer Castrated bull.

stock route A road or track for driving stock. Stock routes used to take mobs of sheep and cattle around the backs of towns and settlements, where they had the right of way over vehicles.

stone-bruise Children went bare-foot, without shoes on the metalled roads, and got bruises which sometimes became infected and had to have poultices put on them, or be lanced.

strainer post A heavy, stayed fence post that takes the strain of the wires, especially at the corner or the end of a fence.

"Strike a light!" Like saying, "Heck!" or "Gee!"

strong-eye A dog, usually a border collie, that can hold sheep with its eye, and control them.

struck, to strike To grow a plant cutting to the stage where it has roots.

stud A little metal device that went through buttonholes and kept your separate collar attached to its shirt.

suet pudding A scrumptious boiled pudding made from flour and white kidney fat.

sugarbag A bag of fine sacking holding 70 pounds or about 32 kilograms of sugar.

swaggers Men without work, carrying their swags and walking the roads.

swing the billy Hang the billy over the fire to make a brew of tea.

taihoa Hold on, take it easy.

tank Most people used to catch the rain off roofs in tanks, for cooking, washing, and drinking.

tankstand The wooden frame that a tank stood upon. It was often enclosed to make a shed.

taradiddle Nonsense.

tatie A potato.

tenner Ten pounds in old money.

Tom Sawyer The boy in *The Adventures of Tom Sawyer* by Mark Twain. It's a marvellous book! Tell your teacher I said she had to read it to you.

tomahawk A small, short-handled axe.

totara A big New Zealand tree. Its red wood was used for piles, the short posts that houses stood upon, because it didn't rot in the ground.

trap Mouth.

Tuppenny A nickname made from tuppence or two pence (pennies) in our old money.

umpteen Lots.

vicar The minister of the local Anglican church.

Waikato Times A Hamilton newspaper.

wash-house An earlier name for a bathroom, usually one that had a bath and hand basin, as well as a copper and tubs for doing the washing.

wax matches Wax matches were easier to light, harder to blow out, and were thought to cause fires, so we stopped making them many years ago.

Weekly News, The Auckland Weekly A magazine very popular throughout New Zealand for its local news and its photographs. It was often used as wallpaper.

wet fly A trout hook made to look like a sunken fly, and usually cast or fished downstream.

whopper A big lie.

works The freezing works where sheep and cattle are killed and their meat frozen.

windy Scared.

yahoos Louts, hooligans.

year dot, **the** A long time ago.